DEMON
DISCORD

Also by
M.J. Haag

Fairy Tale Retellings
(ALL IN THE SAME WORLD)

BEASTLY TALES

Depravity

Deceit

Devastation

TALES OF CINDER

Disowned (prequel)

Defiant

Disdain

Damnation

RESURRECTION CHRONICLES
(hottie demons!)

Demon Ember	*Demon Escape*	*Demon Dawn*
Demon Flames	*Demon Deception*	*Dmeon Disgrace*
Demon Ash	*Demon Night*	*Demon Fall*

DEMON DISCORD

A RESURRECTION CHRONICLES NOVELLA

M.J. HAAG

Shattered Glass
—PUBLISHING—

ISBN 978-1-63869-010-8 (eBook Edition)
ISBN 978-1-63869-011-5 (Paperback Edition)

Editing by The Proof Posse
Cover design by Shattered Glass Publishing LLC
© Depositphotos.com
Version 04.05.2021

To all the deadend relationships and the partners who stay.
You are worth so much more than you believe.

DEMON DISCORD

All Terri ever wanted was a family of her own. Then, her world fell apart in more ways than one. Hellhounds, infected, and food shortages became her primary concern and would have made pregnancy difficult, but not impossible. Until her husband divorces her in a fit of hurt feelings.

Now, she has a choice to make. She can linger in the same house with a man filled with bitter resentment...or find someone in the other survivor settlement to take her in. Someone not human.

The thought of living with a fey makes Terri want to faint with fear, but maybe there's a silver lining. The fey want babies just as badly as she does.

Starting over isn't easy. But it might be exactly what she needs.

CHAPTER ONE

My stomach growled as I stirred the oatmeal. I hated cooking. No, not true. I didn't mind cooking, in general. I only hated not tasting what I was making when I was so damn hungry. Shifting my position, I lifted the spoon to my mouth, quietly blowing on the contents.

"No taste-testing, Terri," Wayne said from behind me. "We don't want the others accusing you of eating more than your share."

Annoyed but hiding it, I nodded and returned to stirring the pot of oatmeal without tasting it. No matter how much I wanted things to be different, Wayne was right.

Tensions were understandably high in Tenacity. People were going hungry, and there weren't any stores to run to for food. Those days were long behind us. Here, in this house protected by a wall of compressed vehicles, we were safely hidden away from what was happening in the world. Hidden, but not ignorant. Wandering humans infected by the plague existed even when we couldn't see them. Or hear them. So did the creatures with glowing red eyes and a deadly bite who started the plague.

I shut off the stove and mentally redirected my darker thoughts to a more pleasant one.

"It's done," I said, removing the stack of ten bowls from the cupboard. We had just enough to feed everyone in the house.

Pausing, I put one back and thought of our missing housemate.

"Have you heard anything about Brooke?" I asked.

"Nothing specific. Aaron's pretty sure she's another female stolen by the fey."

The fey.

I barely suppressed a shiver that wanted to run through me. Even after weeks of catching glimpses of them, I still found the fey terrifying. Unlike most other survivors who found them disturbing, I could see past the fey's grey skin and pointed ears. What I couldn't quite get over was their size combined with their sharp teeth and reptilian eyes. Those three things screamed predator to me.

I'd been present when Mya led a massive group of the fey to the front gate of Whiteman, claiming they had arrived to help. I'd witnessed the way the fey had pulled the heads from the infected with ease and no remorse. Since that day, Mya and Matt had been trying to spread the message that we humans had nothing to fear from the fey. But I'd also been there the night two of their kind had killed a few guards and let in the infected. I knew their true natures.

But the fey's very inhuman physical attributes and killing tendencies didn't turn away everyone. Brooke was a perfect example of that.

"I hardly think she was stolen," I said, tucking a strand of my chin-length brown hair behind my ear. "She walked out of this house pretty willingly every morning." It was her willingness that confused me. How could she possibly be okay spending time with one of them? Not only okay with it, but enjoyed it based on the way I'd overheard her talking to Sam, her roommate. I wasn't sure how Brooke could see past a fey's terrifying features enough to feel an attraction to one of them.

However, that seemed to be the case because she hadn't come home last night.

"Still, if she's not going to come back, she should let us know so Matt can reassign someone to our house," Wayne said.

"You mean someone willing to leave for supply runs."

"Of course I mean that. Do you enjoy going hungry?"

There was a note of disapproval and bitterness in Wayne's voice. Something I'd heard often enough during our seven years of marriage.

"We wouldn't be hungry if more of the people here would leave for supplies."

"No one's stopping you."

I let the words roll off of me. After so many years together, I knew he was deflecting.

"What you're doing is important too, Wayne. I wasn't criticizing. Without the wood you bring back, we'd all be frozen by now."

He went out every day, returning after a few hours with enough wood to keep us moderately warm throughout another night. No one in the house complained about the quantity. We all understood that it wasn't easy to cut wood quickly and quietly. The men sacrificed speed to keep down the sound that attracted the infected. But just imagine how much wood we would have if he spent more than a few hours out there.

It wasn't only Wayne who did the bare minimum. While he left the house for wood, only two other people took turns leaving for supplies. And not even every day. Bobby and Bram each left once a week. Just enough to keep us from starving. Bobby's grandmother never went out. Like the other four women in this house, she could physically leave.

Fear kept us where we were, though. I understood that. However, that didn't make it any easier to accept when my belly was cramping for food.

Abi and Greyly, the little girl Abi had found, came down the stairs. As soon as I saw them, I started ladling the oatmeal into bowls. Eight equal portions and a slightly smaller portion for the child. They'd barely sat down when Bobby, his grandma, and Bram descended as well.

"Sam's coming," Bobby said. "I heard her moving around. Any sign of Brooke?"

"No," I said.

"Instead of worrying about Brooke, we should focus on what's important," Wayne said. "Either of you up for helping me cut some wood?"

"More heat sounds amazing," Abi said. "Greyly was shivering in her sleep last night."

There were no concerned or sympathetic looks to that comment, and I quickly ducked my head to hide mine. It wasn't right that a little girl, no more than four, was underfed and cold.

"I'll go to the shed and get another blanket for her," I said.

Abi shook her head.

"Danielle and I went yesterday. Everyone's having the same problem and had the same idea. There weren't any extra blankets left. Matt said he would ask Ryan to keep his eyes open for more when they go out for today's supply run."

My heart ached as I glanced at Greyly, who was shoveling in her oatmeal, and old resentments resurfaced. I was still bitter at Wayne for getting a vasectomy, even when I'd begged him not to. It didn't matter that the world had gone to shit and had ripped so many families apart. I'd wanted kids of my own, and it festered that we would never have that chance now.

"Then, I'll need to wait in line for whatever tonight's supply run brings in."

Abi gave me a grateful smile as her cousin, Danielle, joined us. The woman's hair was still wet, and I envied her that today was her shower day. By limiting hot water use, the propane tank out back would hopefully last until Matt and Mya came up with a refill plan. It was a smart strategy. I just wished we were one of the houses with the big enough solar panel system to heat our water too. Cool water sponge baths just weren't the same as an actual shower.

As soon as everyone finished, they piled their dishes in the sink for Grandma to wash and got ready to do their part.

We all had our roles. I cooked and traded supplies. Grandma washed dishes and clothes and kept the common areas of the house tidy. Abi and Danielle went out and socialized, gathering information about who needed what, so I knew what to trade. No one had any idea what Bram and Bobby did on the days they weren't out on a supply run, which was Wayne's major source of contention. Why should they get days off when the rest of us couldn't?

I didn't share his attitude. The thought of leaving the protection of the wall terrified me, and I couldn't imagine what it took for Bram and Bobby to leave once a week.

While I went downstairs and took inventory, I listened to Abi, Danielle, and Greyly leave. The house grew quieter as I sorted through a tote of baby clothes. Most people made do with what they could find. But it was common knowledge that a few of the women from Tolerance were pregnant. If that girl Emily came around, maybe I could trade some—

"Hurry up, Terri," Wayne called from upstairs, making me jump.

I took the small pile of onesies and sleepers upstairs, where he paced in the kitchen.

"Baby clothes? Is this town filled with idiots? A baby is the last thing we need. Can you imagine what their crying will attract?"

"Since one of them is close to giving birth, I'm pretty sure the apocalypse didn't play into their decision making," Grandma said dryly before looking at me. "It's a smart idea, Terri. You saw a potential need for what we have, and I hope you're able to make a decent trade for it."

"She wouldn't need to if your grandson pulled more supply runs."

"Wayne," I said with soft warning.

Ignoring me, Grandma turned away from the sink to face Wayne

"If you're not happy about how often he's going out, talk to him. Don't wait until he's gone to complain about it."

Wayne's face grew red, and he opened his mouth, likely to yell, but was cut short by the door opening.

My heart seized when Brooke walked in with a giant fey trailing behind her. His reptilian eyes scanned the room, lingering on each of us before his lips tilted in a predatorial smile.

I shivered.

"If you're here looking for breakfast, you know the rules."

"No, thanks, Wayne. I found something more satisfying." She took the fey's hand and kissed the back of it. "I'm just here for my underwear unless you want to tell me I have to give up my rights to those too."

Wayne made a disgusted sound.

"No one would want your underwear." Shaking his head, he walked past them and out the door.

Brooke looked at me.

"I don't know how you put up with him. He's a real asshole sometimes."

"It's the stress," I answered. "He doesn't like seeing us go hungry or cold."

"Well, I can do something about the one, but not about the other." She reached into her jacket with a smile and pulled out a box of pancake mix. "It's the add water kind."

Grandma took the box and hugged Brooke. "You're good to think of us when some of us don't deserve it."

The dig on Wayne annoyed me. He wasn't perfect by any means, but he was trying to survive, just like the rest of us.

"You're welcome. And don't let Wayne get to you. Traumatic events change people."

I glanced down at the baby clothes to hide my reaction to that and wondered if Brooke would have been so willing to jump into a fey's arms if not for the apocalypse.

"Are those baby clothes, Terri?"

Looking up, I met her gaze.

"Yes."

"According to what Solin told me, there are more than a few hopeful baby-daddies who'd be willing to trade with you for those. They're obsessed with the babies-to-be and would do anything to ensure they have what they need. You'd have to come to Tolerance to negotiate, though."

My gaze shifted to the fey beside her, and a sick feeling settled into my stomach. I knew going to Tolerance meant more than only leaving the safety of the wall. One of the fey would need to carry me there.

CHAPTER TWO

"I'M GLAD YOU AGREED," BROOKE SAID, WALKING BESIDE ME. She carried a small bag filled with her meager possessions. Things that seemed hardly worth coming back for.

"It gives me a little more of a break," she continued. "Solin is a machine in bed. Zero recovery time needed."

"Uh, I'm not sure what to say to that."

She shot me a grin. "I think 'you lucky lady, you,' works well."

Brooke and I weren't far off in age. Maybe a year or two. Yet, I felt like we were on completely different levels. I absolutely wouldn't call hours of sex a good time. The five minutes it took Wayne to finish was more than enough. But I could see the happiness in her expression and couldn't rob her of it.

"I'm glad he found you then."

She laughed. "Oh, no. *I* found *him*. The best decision I ever made was making my move on him. Pay attention when we meet them at the wall. He has a ring on his finger. He wanted it like a fashionista wants purses."

Her genuine joy baffled me.

"So how many human-fey couples are there now? And how many are pregnant?"

"Well, there's Mya and Drav, the OG of human-fey couples, and Solin mentioned maybe a dozen others. Mya's the first and only human-fey pregnancy that they know of. But there's a human who's close to her due date. Obviously, that baby is all human. I honestly wouldn't mind being third on that list."

"Really? You'd want a baby?"

"I know motherhood isn't for everyone, so I'm not judging if that's your angle, but it's mine. Can you imagine a little grey-skinned baby? Or better yet, a fey girl? That child would be so spoiled, it wouldn't even be funny."

"Don't you worry about how you'd provide for a baby or keep one safe? They cry. A lot."

Brooke shrugged lightly.

"Nope. I don't worry about any of that. The way Solin talks, we'll have sitters lined up waiting for a turn until the kid's sixteen. It won't have a chance to cry. And if you saw how stocked Solin keeps his cabinets, you'd get why I'm not worried about food. It might be hard for *us* to get to it, but not them. Considering their burning desire for kids and family, they wouldn't take one on and let them starve. That's just not how they work."

Her face lit up suddenly, and she waved. I followed her gaze and saw three fey waiting by the wall. Even from this far away, I could see how huge they were. Distance blurred their other scary features, but not the memory of the one I'd witnessed pulling the head off of an infected.

One of the three lifted his hand, returning Brooke's

greeting. He didn't move to meet us, though. There were too many people gathered around them, glaring. The fey weren't exactly welcome in Tenacity.

"Solin brought you options," Brooke said in a side whisper. "Isn't that sweet?"

Finding myself the object of intense focus for two fey was far from sweet. I trembled with fear.

"Maybe I should talk to Wayne about this first," I hedged.

"Why? He's the one pushing for you to trade up the stuff in the basement. And we're going to get a far better trade in Tolerance than you will here. Everyone is food-poor."

I knew she was right, but that didn't make it any easier to close the distance between us and the fey. The people glaring extended their hateful stares to us, and I recognized one in the group. Aaron. He gathered wood with Wayne, and like many here, Aaron wasn't a fan of the fey. Which was slightly ironic because rumor had it that he'd been rescued by them. However, unlike many people here, he and his friends were more vocal about their dislike.

His gaze locked with mine, and I saw the surprise flash in his eyes before disgust took over. I quickly looked away.

"I'm Brooke," Brooke said, holding out her hand to the first fey.

"I am Groth," the bigger one said, accepting her hand.

"I am Azio," the second one, only shorter by an inch, said. His gaze was on me.

Brooke glanced at me, too.

"And this is Terri. Terri, pick your ride."

My throat closed as I stared at the pair then slowly shuffled toward Azio. He still towered over me with shoulders that probably brushed the sides of any door he passed through, but smaller was smaller, and I'd take it.

"May I carry you, Terri?" he asked.

My grip tightened on the baby clothes, and I forced myself to nod, but immediately flinched when he moved to pick me up. He paused, and I flushed.

"Would you prefer Groth?" he asked.

My gaze flicked to the other fey watching us.

"N-no," I managed through my tight throat. "You."

He nodded once, his green, vertically slitted eyes watching me closely as he slowly bent to pick me up. He lifted me like I was nothing. The end of the world and the food shortages had done a number on me, but I knew I weighed more than nothing.

"Am I holding you too tight?" he asked, looking down at me.

I shook my head and focused on my hands.

"I won't drop you."

"Okay."

I'd barely managed the words when he leapt up and over the wall. I screamed the whole way.

"You're fine, Terri," Brooke called. "No more screaming, okay? I haven't seen any infected yet and don't want to start now."

Clamping my mouth shut, I nodded and looked around. This was the first time I'd been outside the wall in weeks. It was exceptionally normal looking. Trampled snow filled the quiet clearing. Nothing creepier than the fey lurked nearby.

"I'm sorry for scaring you," the fey holding me said, making me flinch in his arms.

"The jump just surprised me. That's all."

He grunted and looked at the other two fey.

"They're going to run now," Brooke said. "Turn your face toward him so you can breathe and not freeze. We'll be there before you know it."

I nodded and did as she suggested, but with my eyes closed.

A moment later, I felt him moving against me, the barest jostle of his chest against my side. If not for the wind battering the back of my hood, I wouldn't have believed he was running. Within minutes, the cold bit into my jean-clad legs, proving he was though.

I shivered. Then he did the strangest thing ever. He leaned into me, pressing his cheek to the top of my head. I felt...hugged.

The second jump twisted my stomach just as much as the first one had, but I swallowed my scream.

"Would you like to walk now?" the fey holding me asked.

I lifted my head and looked around. There were fey everywhere. Lurking between houses. Stalking along the top of the wall surrounding Tolerance. Hiding behind trees.

"Um...I..."

"I think that's a 'yes,' Azio," Brooke said with a chuckle.

I kept my gaze locked on Brooke as he carefully eased me to my feet, and I tried not to feel the way his hands slid over the backs of my legs or down my arm.

"It's impressive, right?" she asked.

"Huh?"

"This place. I saw the way you looked around. It's so much calmer here—laid back. I went to Jamaica once before the world fell apart. It feels like that. Slower. Calmer."

She motioned for me to walk with her, and I cautiously stepped around my fey-barer to do so.

"I'd never traveled until the evacuation," I admitted. "If not for that, I probably would have died in the town we were born in."

"We?"

"Wayne and me."

"Wow. So high school sweethearts?"

"Yeah. We got married right after graduation. And after that, there was always some reason not to leave," I said.

"That's a shame. There was so much world to see. Not so much, now."

In all honesty, traveling had never interested me. We'd been so busy working and saving so we could fix up our house. If there had been any idle time, I'd spent it on researching items to create a perfect nursery. So many hours wasted.

I closed the door on that bitter thought even as my fingers twitched on the bag of baby clothes. If I had any hope of having children of my own, I would have left these in the basement regardless of how much food I might be able to trade for them. While I put a very high value on the clothes due to what they represented, I knew not everyone saw them in the same light, which meant I would need to take what I could for them and let them go to someone who might someday have a use for them.

"So which of the fey should I talk to about trading?" I asked.

She glanced at Solin. "Do you know?"

"Who wishes to exchange food for baby clothes?" Solin asked.

It'd been a conversational tone, not a yell. So I was completely unprepared for the number of fey who swarmed from everywhere like cockroaches in a kitchen as soon as the lights are turned off.

I stumbled back a step, crashing into one of them.

His grey fingers curled around my upper arms. Heart jackrabbiting in my chest, I tilted my head to look back at my captor and met the unblinking gaze of the fey who'd carried me.

His vertical pupils narrowed. My grandparents had a cat with eyes that did the same thing just before it pounced on its prey.

My throat closed, and my vision tunneled, a sure tell that I was going down.

Oblivion cushioned my fall.

CHAPTER THREE

WARMTH PRESSED AGAINST MY CHEEK, AND I EXHALED HEAVILY, feeling weak and shaky. Rather than opening my eyes, I focused on my breathing, counting the steady in and out rhythm.

"She's waking." The strange masculine voice brought back the memory of exactly why I'd fainted.

"Good. We should still have Cassie look at her."

There was a sharp, rapid knock that tempted me to open my eyes, but I resisted. Someone was carrying me, and when it came to the identity of who, ignorance was bliss. At least until I had a few minutes to recover from the last faint.

"Hey, Cassie," Brooke said. "This is my friend Terri. She fainted."

"Bring her in," the woman replied. "Did she hit her head when she fell?"

Brooke snorted as we moved again.

"Not a chance. Azio caught her before her knees fully buckled."

I could feel my pulse pick up again and forced myself to

think of breakfast. The oatmeal had been so bland the day before. So this morning, I'd tried adding cinnamon and a dash of ginger and nutmeg. It had helped. Sugar would have been better.

"Lay her down here, Azio," Cassie said.

A mattress pressed against my back, and the arms around me disappeared, making it easier to open my eyes.

I found Cassie's worried face, one I remembered from our time in the Whiteman evacuation camp, and stayed focused on her.

"I'm a fainter. I always have been. Usually, I feel it coming and try to get as close to the ground as I can."

"Okay. That's good to know this isn't something abnormal for you. Is there something I can do to help with it? My expertise leans more toward patching up physical injuries."

"No. I should be fine in a few minutes. If I try to sit up too soon or too fast, there's a chance I'll go down again."

"Wow," Brooke said. "You're making it sound like this is a common thing for you. I don't think I've ever seen you faint before, though."

I shook my head.

"It's why I don't go on supply runs or help gather wood. I'm too much of a liability when I get overwhelmed."

Cassie patted my arm.

"You're not a liability. Play on your strengths and hire out your weaknesses."

"Yeah," Cassie agreed. "That's what the fey are for."

My stomach dipped, and my gaze involuntarily moved to the two fey hovering in the door way. I swallowed hard and closed my eyes again.

"Hey, why don't the two of you go help Kerr with the kids? He's supposed to be giving them a bath, but I think he's avoiding putting Caden in the water."

"Babies are slippery when they are wet," one of the fey said.

There was a long moment of silence, then the snick of a door closing.

"You should see Kerr's face when it's bath time. Pure panic. He's terrified he's going to lose Caden under the water even though he only puts three inches in the tub," Cassie said softly before adding, "We're alone. You can open your eyes now."

I glanced at her and Brooke and felt my face flushing. They'd obviously caught on to why I'd fainted.

"How old is your baby?" I asked instead of addressing the elephant in the room.

"He should be around ten months. It's hard to know exactly."

"The days have a funny way of blending into one another now, don't they?" I said.

"They do," she agreed.

Cassie lent me her support as I carefully sat up. My vision stayed steady.

"I'm okay now. Would you know any women interested in newborn baby clothes?" I asked.

"Not really," Cassie said. "Most of the fey with women have been going out for baby supplies on their own. Angel told me that Shax had a whole baby room set up and stocked before she met him. Your best bet is to talk to the single guys."

I looked at Brooke. "Did yours have a room already stocked?"

"Not a room, no. The fey've figured out it makes some women nervous if they come over and see a nursery all set up. He has loads of stuff in the basement. Not food. If you had that, my man would be your guy for trading."

If I had food, I wouldn't have left Tenacity.

"Look, Terri," Brooke said. "I know they freak you out, but they're really nice and wouldn't harm a hair on your head. Just talk to them. You'll see."

"This isn't a social visit. I just want to trade for food and go back before I'm missed."

"Grandma knows where you are," Brooke said. "You won't be missed. Come on. I'll help you negotiate. You might even get a free lunch out of the deal."

We skipped lunch most days in our house, so the possibility of a meal tempted me more than the trade, which would be split nine ways once I returned. Yet, the idea of facing so many of them again set my heart racing.

"I'm not sure I—"

"It won't be a big crowd again," Brooke said quickly. "I think we learned our lesson there. What if we went door to door? Would that be better?"

I flushed at the open acknowledgment of my fear of them.

"Maybe? I don't know." I sighed. "I just don't want to offend anyone." How many times could I rudely faint at the sight of them before they ripped my head off? I shuddered at the memory.

"I have an idea," Cassie said. "Come with me."

I followed her out of the room and up the stairs, where I heard a lot of childish giggling.

"More!" a little girl squealed.

Cassie held her finger to her lips and motioned for me to peek into a doorway. What I saw nearly stopped my heart.

Three of those huge fey were crowded into a modest bathroom. One knelt next to the tub, his hands wrapped around the waist of a little boy, who was grinning up at the foam tower on top of the fey's head.

"More!" the little girl, no more than four, shouted.

One of the fey scooped a handful of suds from the tub and plopped it on the kneeling fey's head. The baby clapped his hands and squealed, kicking the soapy water with his feet. The fey holding him grunted.

"His strength is endless. He will be a fierce fighter when he is grown."

I tried to slowly retreat, but the one who had carried me here looked up just then. Our gazes locked and his pupils did that terrifying narrowing again.

A small sound escaped me.

"Okay, I think that's enough fun time," Cassie said, stepping around me. "Kerr, you have more soap on you than the kids. They need actual washing."

"How can I wash him and hold him at the same time?"

"That's why I sent these two up here. How can three fey not handle two children?" She didn't say it meanly but with a hint of humor-filled exasperation.

"Move over, Papa. Let me show you how it's done."

The one watching me focused on Cassie as she knelt down and started wetting the baby's hair.

"He doesn't like water in his face," the little girl said.

"Exactly," Cassie agreed. "We have to be careful. We don't want Caden to be afraid of bath time."

All the fey watched raptly as she bathed the boy first then the little girl. It didn't take long before the little boy was wrapped in a towel and handed off to the fey who'd carried me and the little girl was delegated to the man beside the tub.

"I want six braids this time," she said, looking him in the eye.

"Is that how we ask, Lilly?" Cassie asked.

"Papa, may I please have six braids?"

She was adorable, and I ached as I watched him nod in agreement. My gaze shifted to the little boy. He and the fey holding him were staring just as raptly at one another. Then, the little boy reached out, took one of the fey's braids, and stuck the leather-wrapped end of it into his mouth.

"He is hungry," the fey said, looking at Cassie. "May I feed him?"

She pried the braid from the boy's grasp. "He's not hungry. He's tired because he was up way too early this morning. Come on, you. Let's get you dried off and put you down for a nap."

With longing, I watched her and the baby leave.

"Feeling better about the situation?" Brooke asked softly beside me.

I understood what she was asking and what Cassie had been trying to do by letting me glimpse this little slice of domestic bliss. However, I'd already known the fey loved children. Who didn't love kids? It was what the fey did with the adults that gave me nightmares.

"I just want to trade food for these baby clothes and go home," I said carefully.

"I will trade with you," the fey who'd carried me said.

"That's great, Azio."

Azio. I needed to remember that. Azio. Azio. Azi—

His gaze met mine, and my mind went blank.

"If you don't mind, Solin and I will tag along to your house, okay?"

The fey grunted, not looking away from me. His pupils narrowed. My throat started to close, and my heart started to race.

Brooke turned me and nudged me down the hall.

"What kind of food are you hoping for?" she asked. "If Azio doesn't have it, I'm sure some other fey will."

Clinging to the change of subject, I took a steadying breath.

"Anything really. Neither Bram or Bobby went out on a supply run today."

"Why didn't Wayne go?"

"He's cutting wood like he always does."

"Right."

Not liking her tone, I gave her a sharp look.

"That was rude of me. I'm sorry. Your husband. Your business."

We left the house in silence, and I'd almost forgotten about the two fey trailing behind us until Brooke asked Azio which house was his.

"This way," he said softly. Rather than leading, he merely pointed and continued to walk behind us along with Brooke's fey.

Eventually, we found our way to a cute brick tri-level

home with faded green shutters and a blue front door. Smoke curled up from the chimney, and my steps slowed as I took in the extensive array of solar panels on the attached garage.

"I bet they never run out of hot water," I said under my breath.

"I don't think anyone here runs out of anything or has to have designated shower or laundry days."

Brooke led the way forward and opened the door for our party. A fey rose from the sofa and paused the movie he'd been watching.

I froze.

"Groth, she fears our eyes," one of the fey behind me said in an angry tone.

The fey staring at me quickly averted his gaze, but it didn't matter. I'd done exactly what I'd feared I would do. I'd offended one of them.

A wave of dizziness washed over me, and I quickly squatted down and set my forehead on my knees. A hand brushed over the back of my head, and I flinched, waiting for the second one to join it.

"I'm sorry," I whispered. "I didn't mean it."

"Terri, it's okay," Brooke said. "I promise."

The hand continued to smooth over the top of my head.

"Let's just get her some food and get her home, okay?" Brooke said.

There was a grunt close to my ear. I jerked my head up and found myself face to face with the fey bent down in front of me. Our gazes met for a second as he continued to pet my hair.

"I wish I had different eyes. I'm sorry they frighten you."

CHAPTER FOUR

His words, along with the regret in which he'd delivered them, humanized him in a way nothing else had. They also caused a wave of shame to wash over me. Could this fey honestly care what I thought of him?

"There's nothing wrong with your eyes," I managed. "And I'm very sorry I gave you that impression. It wasn't intended."

He grunted, stood, and offered his hand.

I glanced up at him in surprise. Intentional or not, his gesture felt like a test to see if I meant what I'd said. However, he quickly turned his head, averting his gaze from my wide-eyed focus. Another nudge of shame prompted me to accept his hand.

My fingers trembled as they slid against his warm palm, and his hold remained light while he helped me to my feet. As soon as I was steady, though, I tugged my hand free.

Brooke watched me with sad disappointment while all three fey did their best not to look at me at all.

"All of the food is in the kitchen," Azio said. "Go look and tell me if any of it interests you."

Likely, it would all interest me, but I didn't say that. Instead, I removed my shoes and hurried across the room to go through his cupboards. He hadn't been kidding about all the food being there. Where most houses had one or two cabinets dedicated to food and the rest chock-full of dishes to prepare them, Azio had done the opposite.

Everything was neatly organized—cans with cans, boxes with boxes, bags with bags, and so forth. My gaze wandered over the quantity in awe. I hadn't seen so much food in one place since my last trip to the grocery store months ago.

I trailed my fingers over an unopened two-pound bag of rice and the dried beans underneath it. Together, they would feed everyone in the house for two or three days. One was hardly worth the clothes I had, never mind both.

A grey hand reached around me and pulled both bags from the cupboard.

"What else would you like?"

I shook my head but didn't turn around. He was too close.

"I can't take more. That's already too much." I opened the bag and started placing the clothes on the counter. Three onesies and three sleepers.

He picked up one item and smoothed it out.

"Caden seems so small already. It is hard to believe they come out even smaller."

"It's a good thing they do, considering where they come out of," Brooke said from behind me with a laugh.

All three fey made odd sounds, and I glanced at Azio,

who was staring at the clothes with a deeply troubled expression.

"Angel said there will be much pain and blood," he said, without looking at me. "Shax is very afraid for her. Many of us are. We want children, but not at the risk of our females."

"There are risks all around us. There could be another breach. We could get sick. Run out of food. Or wood. Or water. There are so many ways we could die. I'd rather die trying to have a baby than not try at all," I said, staring at the clothes.

"You would like children?"

"More than anything. But sometimes, some things just aren't meant to be."

There was a long moment of silence, which I interrupted.

"Are you interested in trading?"

"Yes. I will take the tiny clothes in exchange for these bags."

"Thank you. There are more clothes if you're interested."

"I am."

"Hey, Azio. They typically don't have a midday meal at her house. Would you care if we ate here?"

I turned, staring at Brooke in shock at her blatant self-imposition.

"Please. Eat whatever you'd like," Azio said.

"I can't. You've already given too much."

"They don't mind. I promise," Brooke said, hurrying to join me in the kitchen. "Their idea of cooking is throwing stuff together in a pot. Having us make something for them will help even the trade. Plus, we get to eat well too. What do you want to make us?"

The fey next to Brooke laughed.

"My Brooke does not like to cook. She is trying to trick you into cooking for her."

Brooke grinned at me.

"Every meal you've made has been good, and that was without a stocked pantry. Imagine what you could make here," she said, gesturing to all the food in the cupboards.

A smart person never said no to food.

The fey moved into the living room, far enough out of sight to put to the back of my mind as Brooke and I worked together to make a meal. She mostly talked and fetched while I worked. I didn't mind, though.

It was the most relaxed meal preparation I'd done in months. An honest to goodness chili with chunks of meat, beans, onions, and peppers. The slight wilt to the green pepper hadn't bothered me in the least. And the selection of seasonings Azio had made the chili the best thing I'd tasted in ages.

Brooke was quick to grab a spoon of her own for testing.

"This smells amazing," Brooke said, inhaling. She blew gently to cool her bite then ate it. She groaned as she chewed then swallowed. "Babe, I know you don't like tomatoes, but I swear you have to try this. When all this stuff is mixed together, it's not the regular red stuff."

"I'm sorry," I said quickly. "If I'd known he doesn't like tomatoes, I could have made something different."

Brooke laughed. "None of them like tomatoes. But they like meat. So this is a fifty-fifty shot."

"Oh." I looked down at the pot, a sick feeling settling in my stomach.

"Hey, it's fine. You'll see."

She turned me and steered me to the table, which she

had already set. As soon as I took a seat, the three fey joined us. I kept my eyes on my bowl as Brooke served us all. She filled our dishes to the top and put a small spoonful into each of the fey's bowls.

"Dig in," she said, sitting.

I tentatively took a bite and waited for their reactions.

"You are right, my Brooke. It does not taste like the red sauce in the cans."

"It heats my mouth," the other fey said.

"It does," Azio said. "I like it."

I flushed and smiled down at my bowl, relieved that they'd liked it. Breathing a little easier as they helped themselves to bigger portions, I slowly consumed mine. When I finally scraped the bottom of the bowl, my stomach felt tight and full. I couldn't remember the last time I'd eaten like that, and I thought of little Greyly with guilt.

"You're frowning. Here." Azio slid his partially eaten bowl toward me. "Eat this."

"I swear, I couldn't eat more if I wanted to. Thank you, though."

"Then why do you frown?"

I glanced at Brooke instead of focusing on the fey.

"This is the most I've eaten at one time in forever. I should have thought of Greyly."

"Every time I spent the day here, I should have too," Brooke said. "But I didn't. I don't think that makes either of us shitty people. We weren't purposely withholding anything from anyone. We just didn't think about it."

"But now I have."

"You have," she agreed. "But don't hate yourself for it. Regret is wasted energy. Figure out how to make it right instead." She flashed a smile at me. "Like how I saw the baby clothes and brought you here, knowing you'd find a better trade."

I returned her smile, truly grateful for her help but still wishing for what couldn't be.

"I miss the days of grocery stores. I'd simply run out and buy her a treat. Then again, she wouldn't need a treat from me if we still had stores."

"I have treats," Azio said. "Who is little Greyly?"

"She's a female child from Tenacity. Close to the same age as Cassie's little girl," Brooke said.

Azio grunted and left the table to retrieve a box of chocolate snack rolls from the cupboard.

"These are treats."

I shook my head, and his gaze locked on me. The chili churned in my full belly, and my pulse jumped. But thankfully, my vision didn't tunnel when his pupils narrowed on me. Not taking any chances, I looked down at the table.

"I can't take those." Trading was fine, but if anyone in Tenacity found out that I was taking handouts from the fey, it would cause trouble in so many ways. I didn't want that kind of target painted on our house.

"Then, trade," Brooke said. "Terri will clean up lunch in exchange for one of the packages inside that box."

I quickly agreed and started collecting bowls at Azio's grunt.

"Thanks for the meal, Azio, and for helping us out. And since it looks like you have everything under control here, Terri, I'm going to take Solin home. We have some drawing to do."

She'd barely gotten out the last word when Solin tossed her over his shoulder and strode for the door. Brooke laughed the whole way, waving to me just before the door closed behind them.

Shocked at how quickly she'd left me, I blinked at the door then slowly turned toward the two strange fey lingering by the table.

They both watched me closely.

Azio tilted his head as he studied me.

I started to wheeze in air and spots danced in my peripheral.

Focusing on the stack of bowls in my hands, I hurriedly placed them in the sink then gripped the counter.

I tried to think calming thoughts but could feel the panic taking over and slowly slid to the floor. A hand touched the top of my head.

"You are safe, Terri. I won't let you hurt yourself."

I nodded just before I went under.

When I came to, strong arms held me close to a hard chest. I turned my head into the warmth and did my best not to think. Water was running nearby, and I could smell soap. Both were comfortingly normal.

Something rubbed against the top of my head—a nose?—and the chest of my barer expanded slowly.

"She smells good."

"She does."

My eyes popped open, and my gaze locked onto the fey standing by the sink. He glanced at me and quickly looked away.

"She's awake." He reached into the water and started to wash a bowl.

"I'm supposed to do that," I said.

He nodded, rinsed the bowl, and stepped aside.

"Are you feeling well enough?" Azio asked, his chest rumbling against me as he spoke.

"I think so."

He set me down slowly and waited for me to regain my footing before letting go. Neither spoke as I quickly cleaned up lunch without making any more eye contact. Azio packed my food, including a pack of the snack rolls, in a bag when I finished.

"Will you take me home now?" I asked.

"Yes."

I practically fled the house after putting on my coat and shoes and immediately regretted my hurry. The fey were still everywhere, and the walk back to the wall tested my ability to stay on my feet. By the time we reached it, I was breathing fast.

"May I carry you?" Azio asked.

I didn't hesitate to agree. He picked me up and had me over the wall before I could squeal. I tucked my face against his chest to stay warm. His arms slightly tightened around me and I couldn't say I minded the feeling of being hugged just then. It'd been a long and very stressful morning.

He slowed without jumping, and I lifted my head to see Tenacity's wall in the distance.

Confused and a little worried, I looked up at Azio.

"Will you trade with me again tomorrow?"

Despite my fear, there was only one answer to give.

"Yes."

CHAPTER FIVE

THERE WEREN'T MANY PEOPLE AROUND WHEN I QUIETLY thanked Azio and hurried away with the traded food safely hidden in my jacket. I couldn't decide what I wanted to do first. Go home and show Grandma what I'd managed to get or find Greyly. Part of me was worried that, if I went straight home, anyone there would demand a share of the girl's treat.

Spotting Abi and Greyly lingering near the storage shed saved me from having to make any decision.

"Hi, Terri," Abi said when she saw me. "Any luck today?"

The woman beside her snorted, her humor twinkling in her eyes.

"From what I hear, it wouldn't take any effort to get lucky with the fey."

Abi gave me a confused look.

"I tried trading with the fey. Let's walk home together."

Abi wasn't at all put off by my vague answer or my passive-aggressive demand to go home. She simply nodded and took Greyly's hand. I waited until we were a fair distance away before speaking softly to Abi.

"It went well. It turns out there's a demand for baby clothes over in Tolerance."

"No way. How many women are pregnant over there?"

"Not many. The fey are collecting things in hopes that they'll connect with a woman in the future."

"Wow. Did they have anything good over there?"

"I had chili for lunch. So much that I'm still full."

"You traded for a meal?" she asked with a troubled side-glance at me. "I wouldn't tell the others that."

"It was part of the trade. So was this." I paused and pulled the twin pack of snack rolls out of my jacket. "It's for Greyly. I have rice and beans for everyone, too."

"Terri, that's really sweet to think of her. Are you sure you want to give it to her? It might cause problems."

"I'm positive."

She gave me a grateful smile and opened the package for the little girl. I watched her consume every bite far too quickly and doubted she tasted much of it.

"She shouldn't skip lunch," I said.

"No, she shouldn't. Maybe we could have a house vote on that again."

I nodded, remembering how it had gone the last time. No one wanted to go light on the calories. Neither did they want to run short on food and go a day or two without anything. It wouldn't even be a problem if Bram and Bobby weren't the only ones going out for supplies.

"I'll sort through more of the clothes tonight and go back tomorrow." These trades would never bring home as much as a real supply run would. But maybe I'd stop fainting so much and eventually be able to do my part, too.

"See if you can trade for some cans of veggies. It's been a while." As she spoke, Abi smoothed back Greyly's hair.

The girl gave the woman a small smile as she continued walking.

"I saw a little girl around Greyly's age there. She's part of a mixed family and seemed very happy. Well-fed too. Have you ever thought of...you know?"

Abi chewed on her lip for a minute.

"I have. But I want to make sure I'm making the right choice for everyone involved, not just for Greyly and me."

"Can you afford to be that considerate?"

"I don't want to agree to spend my life chained to someone who's going to treat me like I'm less than."

"Less than what?" Greyly asked, proving she was listening closely.

"Less than the smart, independent survivor that I am." She looked at me. "I want to be valued for more than my parts."

I understood what she meant and nodded. That the fey craved women of their own was common knowledge. The rumor around Tenacity was that the fey had been locked away for eons and were looking for females to fuck now. But if all they wanted was sex, they wouldn't be collecting baby clothes.

Wayne's voice startled me the moment I walked through the door.

"What in the hell were you thinking?" He stood before us with his arms crossed.

Abi and I shared a look, unsure which of us he was

talking to.

"I had to hear from Nat that some grey bastard made my wife squeal."

Understanding he was upset with me, I calmly removed my jacket.

"Do you know how that made me feel, hearing that, Terri? Do you know how it made me *look*?"

"Who cares how it made you look," I said, tossing the bag of rice to him. "I found someone to trade with me. That's all that should matter."

He looked down at the rice he'd caught.

"And what did you have to trade for this?" he asked, his tone flat.

Abi hurried Greyly away as I narrowed my eyes at him.

"Baby clothes. Nothing you have any use for."

His gaze locked with mine.

"A bag of rice and a bag of beans for the baby clothes you had this morning? Even they're not that stupid." He moved closer to me, dropping his voice so the others wouldn't hear him from the kitchen. "I can't believe having a baby means more to you than I do."

I jerked back from him as if he'd slapped me.

"I didn't have sex with anyone, you ass." With the beans in hand, I pushed past him and walked into the kitchen just as Greyly was quietly telling Grandma about the treat I'd given her.

"Where'd she get chocolate?" Wayne asked from behind me.

"From me. And for your information, I cleaned for it. Dishes. Just in case you're thinking I cleaned something else."

"We share what you trade, Terri. Equally."

"No, not equally. Greyly always gets smaller portions."

"Because she's smaller!" he yelled, clearly frustrated with me, which was just fine since I was equally frustrated with him.

"She's growing. She needs more."

"I don't care. We have rules."

"We do," Grandma agreed, speaking up for the first time. "Anyone who leaves the wall shares the supplies they provide as they see fit."

"I'm glad that Terri thought of us at all," Abi added. "Brooke never did."

"Fine," Wayne snarled. "I see how this is going to be. Enjoy your food."

He slammed the door on his way out of the house.

"He didn't bring back any wood," Grandma said. "Once they told him you were gone, he came back here."

"I'm sorry."

"Don't be. I sent Bobby for wood. He hates listening to those narrow-minded men, but it's better than freezing."

I SAT at the kitchen table, a bowl of beans and rice in front of me. The rest of the house was quiet as I waited for Wayne to come home. When he did show up, he leaned against the door frame and scowled at me.

"We saved you your equal share," I said, sliding the bowl toward him. "We also voted that Greyly should get a lunch. Just her. Just her normal small portion."

"Doesn't count. We weren't all present."

"Whose fault is that? You're the one that stormed off in a fit."

"A fit? You left with another man. What was I supposed to think?"

I shook my head at him.

"Since you're the one who suggested I try to trade what's in the basement for food, you were supposed to have faith in me. I did exactly what you wanted. Unlike you."

He threw his hands up in the air again. "Here we go. Are you going to hate me forever because I was man enough to stand up for what I wanted? A life without being chained down."

"If you didn't want to be chained down, then why did you want to marry me?"

"Back then, you were good at giving head."

"Back then, I liked you more."

He snorted.

"Don't worry. I won't be touching you again until I know for sure you're not carrying some grey abomination in your baby-hungry uterus."

I busted out laughing. "Baby-hungry uterus?"

"I see the way you look at that kid. Being around her isn't helping you. We'll talk to Matt and transfer to another house. One without kids."

I stood and shook my head. "Being around her isn't helping you. Sleep on the couch tonight. It'll be more comfortable for you."

"Already planned on it," he said as I walked away.

I slept fitfully despite having the bed to myself. Even in my sleep, I was angry at Wayne. I couldn't believe he had actually accused me of cheating on him. I'd forgiven his initial reaction, figuring he'd said what he had out of fear for my safety after hearing I'd left. But I was struggling to forgive everything he'd said when he'd come home.

He could be such a stubborn ass at times.

Telling myself that didn't ease the sting of his accusation, though. Baby-hungry uterus? Who said that? A man afraid of kids, that's who. The anger and bitterness continued to climb until I gave up sleeping at dawn and got out of bed to use the bathroom.

Wayne didn't move on the couch as I let myself downstairs. He snored with the ease of an untroubled soul, which only annoyed me more.

In the basement, I started the process of sorting through clothes. Some of it was too cute to giveaway yet. I removed a few items too impractical to keep, like a tiny dress with more frills and ruffles than a quinceanera gown. The fey probably wouldn't trade for it, but there was no harm in trying.

With six items neatly packed away in a plastic bag, I went upstairs to start breakfast. At the first clang of the pot, Wayne roused and joined me in the kitchen. He didn't apologize for being a dumbass, though, so I remained quiet.

Breakfast proceeded like the day before, and as soon as the dishes were in the sink, I grabbed the bag of clothes.

"You're not going back there," Wayne said, noticing.

"You're telling me you don't want me to do my part?"

"No, do your part. Here. With your own kind."

Grandma muttered "pigheaded" under her breath as she washed. The others hurried to clear out of the house.

"There's no food here, Wayne. I'm not going to pass up the opportunity to trade for food because you're insecure."

"I'm not insecure. I'm disgusted. Unless you walked, you let one of them touch you. You leave again, and I won't be able to ignore that. You leave, and we're done."

I could see in his eyes that he meant every word he was saying, and a sick feeling settled in my stomach. Anger, fear, and unimaginable hurt consumed me.

"Can you even hear yourself? You're telling me to choose between you and food?"

"I guess I am. Or maybe I'm asking you to choose between me and living here. Let's move to another house filled with people more able to carry their weight. There'd be no need to trade then."

Grandma snorted.

"Do you have any idea how stupid you sound? How do you think Bram and Bobby return from those supply runs with food? The fey. That's how. The big men touch every single item, packing it up and carrying it to the trucks, then unpacking it again when it gets here. Bram and Bobby are only there to point out what's useful. Stop being a hypocrite. What Terri is doing is just as useful. Why do you always have to find ways to put her down?" Grandma turned on me. "Honey, even at the end of the world, you could do a lot better than this man."

I blinked at the intensity in Grandma's voice.

Wayne snorted. "Spoken like a true man-hater."

Grandma threw the rag in the water and stalked off to her bedroom, leaving Wayne and me alone.

"You leave, then don't bother coming back."

I calmly put on my jacket and walked out the door.

CHAPTER SIX

Ignoring all the hate-filled glares sent his way, Azio waited for me near the wall. He watched my approach with keen attention that I didn't immediately notice. I was too busy silently fuming.

"Good morning, Terri. May I carry you?" he asked.

"You may."

It wasn't until we were over the wall that I realized leaving with him hadn't been necessary. I knew the contents of his cupboards and could have negotiated a trade without leaving Tenacity. But staying would have felt like I'd let Wayne win. And he'd already had far too many wins in our marriage.

Rather than asking Azio to turn around, I tucked my face against his chest. His arms tightened around me slightly just as they had the day before. And darn if I didn't like it. I pretended it was the hug I was craving at the moment—comfort from someone who cared.

That thought made my eyes water, and I sniffled.

"You are safe, Terri," Azio said a moment before he jumped, and my stomach flipped.

He didn't put me down as soon as he landed, though. I was smart enough not to look up this time.

"May I carry you to my house? I don't want you to faint again."

"That's very considerate. Thank you."

He didn't move.

"Is that consent to carry you?" The hesitance and confusion in his tone had me smiling.

"It is. Thank you for double-checking."

This time he started walking, and I kept my forehead pressed against his tee-shirt-covered pectoral until he reached his front door. He let me down without me having to ask.

Inside, the same fey from the day before watched a movie, which he paused when I entered.

He didn't look up at me, though.

"Good morning, Terri," he greeted.

"Good morning. It's Groth, right?"

"Yes."

Not sure what more to say, I plucked open the bag to show them the clothes. As soon as the dress lay on the back of the couch, Groth stood and came closer. Their expressions ranged from confusion to awe the longer they studied it.

"Babies wear this?" Azio asked.

"Yes. Well, female babies do. Although, I don't think anyone would say anything if you put it on a boy except maybe, 'cute girl.' It's not something a baby would wear every day. It's a special occasion kind of thing. A fancy dress fit for a princess."

"Special," Azio said, petting a ruffle. "I will trade much food for this."

I cringed and felt a stab of guilt.

"If you're looking for clothes, it's better to trade for practical items. Durable outfits." Which I'd brought with and quickly produced. Azio considered the little jeans. Without looking at me, he grunted and went to the kitchen.

I glanced at Groth, who quickly looked away from me.

"Do you have another one like this? I would like one too."

"There are other dresses, but none like this. I can check with other houses, though."

"Thank you."

Something heavy thumped down on the counter in the kitchen, startling me. When I looked over, Azio's gaze locked with mine, and I quickly looked down at what he'd moved. The white paper package confused me for only a moment.

"Is that meat?"

"Yes. Steak, I think. I will give you four more in exchange for all of the clothes."

I wanted to say yes so badly, but I couldn't cheat him like that.

"Honestly, Azio, one steak is more than these clothes are worth."

"To you, maybe. To me, they mean everything."

I risked a peek and quickly averted my gaze at the intensity in his eyes. It made my heart race in fear and in pity.

"You'll need more than clothes to make a baby," I said.

He grunted.

"Why do females fear us?" Groth asked. "We hide our teeth. We look away." He exhaled heavily. "Will you teach us how to be better?"

"Better?"

"Better males to attract females."

He won my attention and quickly looked away, which made me feel all kinds of guilty even as I was relieved.

"The problem isn't with the fey. We just need more time to get used to you. We've all had our lives turned upside down since those earthquakes. The infected. The hellhounds. Winter. Food shortages. It's been one bad thing after another. It's hard to focus on relationships with all of that going on." As I said it, I thought of Wayne. There was so much pressure on him. On us both. Was it any wonder we were both snapping at each other?

"Will you tell us more about what's changed?"

"The clothes and conversation in exchange for the steaks?"

"Yes."

My stomach twisted at the idea of spending hours alone with two of them, but that white-wrapped package wrapped sang its siren song loud enough it drowned out enough of my fear that I was actually considering it. It wasn't like I had anything better to do, and there was a couch nearby if I ended up fainting again.

"It's a deal," I said, taking off my jacket.

I talked about life before the quakes and the hardships we'd faced since then. Azio got up after a while and brought me a glass of water. I smiled my thanks and continued explaining. When he directed me to sit at the table, I did and watched him start to make something as I kept talking.

He and Groth both asked questions. During the entire conversation, they were polite and listened attentively. We paused to eat the stew Azio had prepared for us then they sat at the table while I did the dishes.

"So only two of the men in your house leave for supplies?" Azio asked. "And only once every three days?"

"Yeah. It makes meals like this one even more special. Thank you for feeding me."

"Thank you for talking to us."

"Of course. If it's all right with you, I should go home now."

Like when I'd arrived, he carried me as soon as we left the house so I wouldn't freak out. Then he ran all the way to Tenacity before slowing and asking me the same question as the previous day.

"Will you trade with me again tomorrow?"

I thought of all the clothes still in the basement and the steaks weighing down the backpack he'd provided me. It would be foolish to pass up a chance to trade for more food. Yet, I hesitated. I was growing more comfortable around Azio and Groth, and that terrified me because of the promise I'd made to myself. Once I was comfortable, I'd pull my own weight and go on supply runs.

Azio exhaled heavily and set his head on top of mine. Oh, how I liked that simple, comforting move.

"I'm sorry I scare you."

"And I'm sorry I'm not better at hiding it. You shouldn't feel guilty about my shortcomings. I'll trade with you tomorrow and every day afterward for as long as I can find clothes. Deal?"

"Deal."

"And for the record, I don't think I'll always be afraid of fey. Spending time with you is helping."

This time, his hug wasn't nearly as subtle, and I grinned into his chest, only feeling a smidge of guilt for the contact. Yes, I was married. But I wasn't doing anything wrong. I wasn't having improper thoughts. And considering the questions they'd asked me today, neither Azio nor Groth were having improper thoughts. They were simply curious about humans in general.

Azio jumped over the wall and deposited me inside before leaving. I hurried home, anticipating the stunned reactions of my housemates and husband when I showed them what I'd obtained. However, when I arrived home, I didn't receive the greeting I expected.

The meager pile of my possessions waited on the table along with Wayne's wedding band. He'd smashed it flat, so it wasn't wearable anymore.

Setting the backpack aside, I picked up his ring, too dazed to know what to think. In all our years together and all our fights, even the one about the vasectomy, he'd never taken it off.

A slight sound from the doorway leading into the kitchen let me know I wasn't alone.

"I'm sorry, honey," Grandma said softly.

"Where is he?"

She shook her head slightly, and I narrowed my eyes.

"Wayne, don't you dare hide from this."

Grandma stepped back, and Wayne strode in.

"I'm not hiding. I was giving you a chance to leave quietly."

"I'm not leaving." I grabbed the backpack and opened it

to dump the three packages of steak on the table. "Real meat, Wayne. That's what I brought to the table. What did you bring, other than a smashed ring and a temper tantrum?"

His face flushed red, and his hand snaked out to grab mine. I was so shocked by the aggressive move that I didn't understand what he was going after until he started tugging on my rings. They hit my knuckle before I thought to fist my hand.

Wayne pried at my fingers, and I hit at his shoulder as he bent over my hand.

"What is wrong with you?" I demanded.

"Nothing. It's what's wrong with you."

He won the rings free and immediately backed away.

"You're not the woman I married anymore, and this is as close to a divorce as we can get."

"Those aren't your rings. Those are mine from my grandmother because you were too broke to buy me anything, remember?"

His eyes narrowed, and he tossed them at me. They pinged off my chest and fell to the floor.

"At least I didn't throw them in your face like you seem to enjoy doing," he said.

My lips trembled as I bent to pick up the rings, but I refused to give in to my tears. Divorced. My insides felt like they were bleeding. After everything I'd done and given up for him, he wanted to divorce me at the end of the world? Where had I gone wrong? What was wrong with me?

"I'll move my things in with Sam," I said, scooping up my pile of clothes.

"Unbelievable. Sticking around isn't going to change my mind," Wayne said.

"The housing is assigned. Where else do you think I can go? I'm just as much stuck with you as you are with me."

"Why don't you run off with one of your fey? Brooke found somewhere else to live easily enough."

My mouth dropped open, and before I could figure out how to reply to that, he stormed out the door.

Grandma sighed heavily and wrapped me in a hug as my tears finally let loose.

"I know that it doesn't feel like it now," she said, "but this moment might be the start of a better future."

I snorted messily and pulled back to wipe at my face.

"How?"

"Wayne is an ass and getting worse by the day."

"It's the pressure."

"No, it's the people he's associating with. A group that hates the fey so blindly that they'd cut their own mothers from their lives to prove they want nothing to do with those grey demons. Not my words. Something Nat's been whispering in some ears."

"And Wayne's mixed up with them? Then he needs help."

Grandma shook her head slowly, her face conveying her disappointment.

"He's not an addict needing intervention. He's a grown man who's choosing hate over love. Don't give any more of yourself to him than you already have, honey."

"What am I supposed to do?"

"Exactly what he said. Look at who brought you home

these last two days. Why stay here when you can live better over there?"

I swallowed hard and looked down at my hands. The left one now bare of rings.

"The rest of you need food too. What about—"

"We'll be fine. The food will stretch further without an extra mouth."

That hurt. But I understood what she meant.

"Make sure Greyly gets bigger portions."

"I will."

CHAPTER SEVEN

THE TIGHTLY PACKED BACKPACK I CARRIED STUCK OUT LIKE A sore thumb as I made my way to the wall. At least, that was what I told myself to explain why people kept looking at me. They were absolutely not staring at my face, which was puffy from a long night of silently crying and very little sleep.

Sam had been kind enough to wake me at dawn, so I wouldn't miss meeting up with Azio. Considering what I planned to ask him, I still wasn't sure if I was thankful for her wakeup or not.

Through my pain, I'd spent a good deal of time last night giving a lot of thought to the future. At first, it had looked bleak and terrifying. While Grandma had been sure that Azio and Groth would welcome me into their home in exchange for baby clothes, the idea of living with two of them had made my vision swim more than once. But then, as I'd sorted the baby clothes after dinner, I'd found a silver lining.

The fey wanted babies. Badly. So did I.

I'd been worried about how long Azio and Groth would let me stay with them and feed me in exchange for the clothes. But if I was pregnant with one of their babies, I'd be set for life.

All I had to do was proposition one of them and not pass out. My vision started to tunnel, and I had to pause and crouch in the middle of the street so I wouldn't faint. Rather than hating Wayne or dwelling on what I'd need to do with one of the fey, I focused on the end result.

A cute, tiny baby.

What wouldn't I do to have one of my own?

Yet, my stomach continued to churn with nerves once I reached the wall. I watched the fey arrive and leave again for the daily supply run and gave Bobby a sad smile when he waved and said goodbye to me. A few minutes later, Azio appeared.

My knees went weak, and I immediately crouched.

"Terri, you are safe," Azio said, hurrying to me instead of waiting for me to come to him.

His hand settled on my head, grounding me. Despite witnessing fey pull heads off of the infected, Azio had never used that strength against me. He was flawlessly gentle, physically and emotionally. I needed to keep reminding myself of that.

"I know," I said, breathing through the wave of panic-induced dizziness. "I'm sorry."

"May I carry you?"

I nodded and leaned into him once he had me in his arms.

We didn't speak as he raced toward Tolerance, which was fine by me. It gave me a few moments to consider how I wanted to broach such a sensitive subject. He jumped the wall and slowed but didn't offer to put me down until we stood on his stoop.

"Thank you," I said when he opened the door for me.

Groth was once again watching a movie, which he immediately paused.

"I have a lot more with me today," I said after removing my shoes and jacket.

They both watched with interest as I went to the dining table and started laying out clothes. I'd taken all of my personal favorites from the basement, including an adorable little ballcap.

Azio immediately reached for it. "I will give you all the food in this house in trade for this hat."

"It is adorable, isn't it? But trust me. It's not worth that much. A baby will outgrow it before it's worn more than a dozen times. Besides, I'm not interested in food this time."

Azio lifted his gaze to meet mine. I forced myself to hold it even as my heart started to pound, and I grew lightheaded.

"What do you want?"

"I'd like to trade all of these clothes in exchange for living here for a few days. Maybe a month if you think that's fair."

His gaze flicked to Groth, then down to my hand.

"Where are your marriage rings?" The slow way he asked made my stomach dip.

"My husband, ex-husband, removed them. He doesn't want to be married to me anymore, which is why I need to find a new place to live."

Azio's pupil's narrowed, and his expression changed from

calm to filled with rage. It was the first time I'd ever seen one of them angry. Even when they were killing infected, they didn't look as mad as Azio did now. More fear pooled in my middle at the thought I'd committed a cultural faux pas that would require immediate death by head removal.

My knees buckled, and I would have gone down if he hadn't moved with frightening speed.

His arms wrapped around my torso, and he pulled me to his chest instead of picking me up like he usually did. Firmly pressed against him, I trembled and struggled to breathe.

"I'm sorry, Terri. Forgive me," he murmured into my hair.

"For what?" I rasped, already imagining what he was about to do.

"Scaring you."

My spiraling panic froze, and I managed to lift my forehead from his shirt. But no farther. I was too afraid of what I might see if I looked up.

"I don't understand," I said, staring at the fabric.

"I am very angry, but not at you. Never you. My anger is for the human males who have so little regard for the opportunities we fey would die to have."

"Is your ex-husband why you fear males?" Groth asked. "Did he hurt you?"

I could hear the promise of retribution in Groth's tone, and with wide eyes, I finally looked up at Azio.

"Wayne never hurt me. Well, he hurt my feelings." I glanced at Groth, who stood nearby. "But Wayne never hit me if that's what you meant."

Azio's hand moved slightly against my back.

"Tell us why we make your heart race and skin reek of fear," he said, his tone once more calm and gentle.

I frowned up at him.

"I stink? Please put me down."

He immediately complied, but I saw the reluctance in his expression.

"I like how you smell under the fear."

I opened my mouth to address that but then shook my head.

"Okay...I feel like we've gone way off-topic. Can I live here with you guys for a while in exchange for the baby clothes?"

"You can live here as long as you want in exchange for nothing but your company," Azio said.

"Oh," I said, stunned. His answer was better than I'd hoped for. It bought me some desperately needed time because I was far from ready to proposition one of them to secure a place to stay. "Can the clothes be in exchange for feeding me then?"

Azio grunted, and I couldn't be sure if it was in agreement or denial. Rather than pressing the issue, I addressed the more immediate question.

"Where should I put my things?"

Azio gave me a tour of the house while Groth trailed in our wake. It was a little nerve-wracking, but I managed without needing to stop. The kitchen was on the ground level with a living room, bathroom, and utility room. A larger family room, bathroom, and two bedrooms were on the lowest split level. And three bedrooms and a bathroom were on the highest level. Overall, it was a comfortably laid out, large house.

"You can choose which bedroom you want," Azio said when we returned to the kitchen.

"Thanks. Is it all right if I shower?"

"This is your home now. There are no rules. You may do what you would like."

I nodded and grabbed my things from the table. As soon as I started up the stairs, the movie began to play quietly again—a sweet romance. I paused on the top step to make sure my ears weren't lying. They weren't. Both fey were intently watching the screen as the woman spoke to the man.

"She looks at his eyes," Groth said.

"She does," Azio agreed.

Knowing they were comparing her to me didn't sit well. I hated that I fainted at the drop of a hat during stressful moments. Okay, not stressful. Terrifying moments. And I hated that I was so afraid of the fey. But couldn't they see I was trying to overcome that? I was here. That was a step, no matter how small.

Hurt by the perceived judgment so soon after Wayne's abandonment, I took the first room at the top of the stairs and gathered what I'd need for a shower. Azio's comment about smelling like fear really bothered me, and I was looking forward to smelling like nothing but me.

I let myself into the shared bathroom and quietly locked the door before starting the shower. The hot water was magical. I soaped and rinsed everything twice, then reluctantly turned the water off.

Wrapping one of the soft, clean bath towels around my

torso, I used my hand to wipe the steam from the mirror and studied my light brown eyes. They weren't as puffy but watered just as easily as they had before the shower when I dwelled on my circumstances.

Instead of dwelling on the unknowns, I finger-combed my brown hair, then dressed in soft lounge pants. They were the only other option to the jeans I'd worn here. I didn't have much. Not anymore. Things tended to be left behind when running for one's life.

Balling up all my dirty clothes, I went downstairs to test if Azio had meant what he'd said. Neither he nor Groth paused the movie when I passed through the room, but I could feel their gazes on me until I disappeared down the hall leading to the utility room. There, I tossed my things into the washer and took the time to handwash my only bra. It'd been ages since it had seen soap because I'd been unwilling to leave the house without it.

In theory, that wasn't a problem anymore since I no longer needed to leave the house.

Distracted by the task and my thoughts, I didn't realize I wasn't alone until I hung the bra on the drying rack and turned to leave. Only Azio's quick reflexes stopped me from face-planting in his chest.

My forward momentum against the hands he clapped down on my shoulders jerked me in place, making my breasts bounce. His gaze locked onto the motion, and his pupils narrowed before expanding to an almost circular shape.

"I'm not afraid of men," I blurted. "I'm afraid of what the fey are capable of."

Azio lifted his gaze to mine, blinked at me, and slowly

released my arms.

"I don't understand."

"I was there at the gates when the fey first came to Whiteman and again when the infected breached the fences." I dropped my gaze to his chest and crossed my arms around myself. "I saw how easy it is for your kind to remove heads. Humans are nothing to you. We're weak. Pathetic. The fey have been patient with us so far. But what happens when we do something you don't like?"

Azio chuckled. Nothing dark and sinister but thoroughly amused.

"Like shoot us?" he asked, lifting his shirt to point to a scar along his ribs. "The human who did this lives. Humans do many things we don't like. We don't kill smart ones. Only stupid ones."

"Shooting you seems pretty stupid."

He grunted and tugged his shirt back into place.

"Can I ask you something?" he asked.

"Sure."

"You seem to fear us more than most humans. Groth thinks your fear will drive you to choose a different home."

I waited for more, but he remained silent.

"That wasn't really a question."

"Will you give us a chance to be less scary?"

That simple question shifted something inside of me, and I looked up at Azio, seeing him as a man for the first time. A broad forehead with dark, arched brows, and thick eyelashes complemented his strong nose and curved bottom lip. If I could figure out how to ignore his terrifying eyes, I'd find him very handsome.

"That's why I'm here," I said, answering him.

CHAPTER EIGHT

GIVING THEM A CHANCE MEANT MOVIE TIME. AND SINCE I SAT between the two, I got to hold the bowl of popcorn. It wasn't some microwaved stuff but honest to goodness theater popcorn with the salt and oil and everything. And I couldn't stop snacking on it as we watched the animated movie Groth had picked.

I shifted my position and tucked my cold feet underneath me, careful not to spill the popcorn. Azio and Groth would help themselves to a piece every now and then, but they didn't eat nearly as much as I did.

Between the cartoon playing on the screen and the food at my fingers, I was relaxed enough that I didn't overthink my moderately sandwiched position.

"Jessie told Byllo that fish are not smart enough to talk here. We can still eat them," Groth said.

"We don't kill smart things," Azio added.

They'd been making commentary since they'd lured me to the couch with popcorn. I didn't mind the conversation. It was insightful hearing how the fey thought. Or, more importantly, the direction of their thoughts, which revolved around feeding me and helping me not be afraid of them.

"See? Not all creatures with sharp teeth are bad," Groth said.

A few moments later, that changed onscreen, and Groth cringed. Hiding my smile, I consolingly patted his knee.

"That doesn't mean you're wrong. The shark just made a mistake."

He glanced at my hand on his knee, and I quickly removed it.

"Sorry."

"Kindness deserves no apologies," Groth said. "You're the first female to touch me. Thank you."

"You're welcome?"

Azio chuckled beside me at the confusion in my voice.

"You don't see it as the gift it is. You will."

Rather than sort out what he meant, I focused on the movie. By the time it finished, I'd eaten all the popcorn, and lunch was the last thing on my mind. Yet, it was on Azio's.

"Come. I will make your midday meal."

I stood and followed him to the kitchen.

"Honestly, I'm not that hungry right now."

"Popcorn is a snack. Not a meal. Jessie told Byllo. You need to eat a variety of healthy food, or you will get sick."

I slowly sat at the table and watched him move around the kitchen with determination.

"If you really want to feed me, I'm not going to argue." I doubted I would ever be able to argue with him.

"What kinds of foods do you like to eat?" he asked.

"All kinds. I'm not picky."

"Were you picky before the hellhounds came?"

"Maybe, but in a different way. I wanted to eat whatever I was craving at the moment."

He paused opening a can of soup and looked up at me.

"What are you craving now?"

"Now? Nothing, really. I'm too full of popcorn. It was too good to stop." I smiled at him because he'd been the one to make it for me. He didn't return my smile. Instead, he grunted and went back to opening the can of soup.

I was still wrapping my head around the fact that I wasn't leaving in a few hours. That this would be my home now. With two fey. It wasn't as terrifying a thought as it had been when I'd arrived.

In short order, the three of us were eating together at the table. It was as quiet as meals back in Tenacity but not as rushed.

"I've noticed some things and was wondering if I could ask a question that might sound judgmental but isn't meant that way," I said after a few swallows of soup.

"You may ask us anything," Azio said.

Groth grunted in agreement.

"Every time I've been here, Groth's watching T.V., and you're never in any hurry to leave. Do either of you have jobs or do something during the day?"

They were both silent for a moment.

"We help with supply runs when it's our turn. If Drav asks for volunteers, we volunteer. Sometimes we watch the other females learn to fight."

I could tell by the way Azio spoke, he was trying to think of more.

"I watch movies to learn human culture," Groth said.

It was on the tip of my tongue to tell him that cartoons

weren't a great representation of that but stopped myself. Most of the animated movies still had lessons about kindness, friendship, and being helpful. Those weren't bad traits to instill in men who liked ripping off heads.

"Back in Tenacity, I was the house cook for breakfast and dinner. I spent my time in between meals trying to trade for additional food. I was just curious what I'll be doing here to keep busy."

"Anything you want to do," Azio said.

I'd been afraid of that answer. I tended to think a lot when I was idle.

We spent the rest of the afternoon watching more movies. They were entertaining enough, but my mind kept drifting to Wayne and how he'd treated me. Or how I'd treated him. Had I been bitter and thrown the vasectomy in his face? Not intentionally. But I hadn't ever managed to make peace with it. Part of me thought maybe I should have. Then I would wonder why I thought my feelings on the matter should count less than his.

Round and round my thoughts went, dwelling the longest on the uncertainty of my future. How long until the fey tired of my company? Would it be smarter to offer to have someone's baby now instead of waiting until the moment they decide to kick me out?

I caught myself spiraling in guilt, regret, and fear and forced myself to pay attention to what Groth and Azio were saying about the movie.

By the time the sun set and the wall lights turned on, I needed a better distraction and asked if I could make dinner. There were more packages of meat in the freezer, one of which I set to thaw for the next day.

Cooking with both of them watching my every move wasn't as nerve-wracking as it could have been. They peppered me with questions about what I was doing and why I was doing it. Especially when I started using the spices they had in the cupboard. It turned into a mini cooking lesson that I thoroughly enjoyed.

I was no master chef by any means, but I knew how to spice up most dishes to make them taste better. Azio and Groth seemed to agree when they took their first bites.

After another quiet meal together, I did the dishes with Azio's help then excused myself for an early night.

Alone in the relative darkness of my room, I thought I would dwell on everything that had happened to me. Instead, the combination of a full belly while snuggled in a warm and comfortable bed immediately pulled me under.

Wayne plagued my dreams. In one, he held me lovingly while telling me that he no longer wanted me as his wife. The contradiction between his actions and his words tore at me. The dreams grew steadily worse until the final one where he promised we'd be a family then threw our baby out the window.

Ripped from the dream, I sat up, heart thundering, unable to shake the anguish I felt for that imaginary child.

"It was a dream," a voice said softly from the dark. "You are safe, Terri."

I placed Azio's voice before I saw his shadow in the doorway.

"Did I wake you?" I asked, struggling to calm down.

"No. I haven't slept yet."

I exhaled heavily and rubbed a hand over my face.

"Do you dream when you sleep?"

"Yes."

"Do you ever have bad ones?"

"Many."

"I hate those kinds. I'd rather have the good ones." I scooted myself back, so I was sitting against the headboard.

"What are your good dreams?" he asked.

I opened my mouth to answer, but before I could, another thought struck me. The door hadn't been open when I'd gone to bed. I'd made sure to close it. And lock it.

"How did you open my door?"

"With my hand?"

His confusion only increased mine. I had locked it. Hadn't I?

"Okay. Why did you open my door?"

He remained quiet.

"You told me you wanted me to give you a chance to be less scary. I'm trying to figure out what non-scary purpose you had for coming into my room in the middle of the night."

"You were very quiet. I needed to see you."

"Were you worried I'd left? In the middle of the night?"

He grunted, and I couldn't tell if he was agreeing or just making noise.

"That would be the same level of stupidity as trying to shoot one of you. I'm not that stupid."

"You're not stupid at all. You're beautiful."

His words were equally worrisome and flattering.

"You do know that how someone looks has nothing to do with how smart they are, right?"

He grunted again, and I was beginning to think he did

that when he disagreed with what I was thinking but didn't want to say so. Instead of finding it annoying, it amused me.

"Well, I promise never to sneak off in the middle of the night. Does that put your mind at ease?"

He gave a very human shrug.

"What would put your mind at ease?" I asked, trying to find a compromise.

"If you slept with the door open."

"I closed it to feel safer."

"I will keep you safe."

A snort almost escaped me since I'd closed the door to keep myself safe *from* him.

"I'd feel more comfortable and sleep better if the door was closed."

He grunted again and reached up to rub the back of his neck.

"Will you tell me about your good dreams?" he asked hesitantly, bringing us back to his original question.

Unwilling to push my point and upset him, I let go of his invasion of my privacy.

"Now, my good dreams are usually about the past. Simple moments that I'll probably never see again, like going to work and talking with co-workers. Grocery shopping." My heart started to flutter, and I forced myself to say the final one. "Having kids."

He tilted his head, and although I couldn't see him clearly, I felt studied.

"How many children do you want?"

"As many as I can have," I said honestly. "I know it's not safe. There are no doctors to help with complications and things out there that want to eat anything that moves. My head knows that. But my heart just wants a family."

"But not with your human man."

I shook my head slowly, feeling sad and bitter and scared.

"No. Not with Wayne. He made it clear years ago that he didn't want kids." I drew my knees up to my chest and picked at the blanket covering me. "In a way, it's a relief he told me to leave. Maybe now I have a chance, you know?" I wasn't sure if I was convincing Azio or myself that it was a good thing.

"You still miss him."

"I was with Wayne for years. Since high school. He was familiar. It's easy to miss what was familiar. But that doesn't mean we were right or happy together."

"And you want to be happy."

"Doesn't everyone?"

Azio grunted again, softer, and reached for the door.

"Sleep, Terri. You are safe."

He closed the door, leaving me alone. Oddly, I didn't feel safer, just lonely and sad.

CHAPTER NINE

It took forever to fall back asleep after Azio left, and dawn came far too soon. Exhausted but knowing I needed to get up, I stumbled from bed. It was only when I reached for jeans that weren't there that I remembered I had no reason to get up so early.

For a brief moment, my heart ached for what I'd lost. I pushed that aside and focused on what I'd gained. I was free to sleep in as late as I wanted, or I could shower first thing in the morning like I used to do before the world fell apart.

Torn, I hesitated for a moment before the urge to shower won. I was already out of bed, anyway.

I went downstairs for the clothes I'd washed and found my jeans and shirt folded neatly on the dryer. However, the bra and yesterday's underwear were missing. Frowning, I started searching the laundry room for them.

"Terri, would you like eggs for breakfast?" Azio called from the kitchen.

That brought an immediate stop to the search. It'd been ages since I'd had eggs.

When I entered the kitchen, Azio's gaze dipped to my chest, which was moving a bit too freely in my rush to verify he had honest to goodness farm fresh food.

"Are you serious about the eggs?" I asked, fighting the urge to cross my arms.

He lifted his gaze and nodded. His direct attention made my pulse leap, but it wasn't enough to distract me from what he'd said.

"Then, yes, please. I'd give anything to have eggs again." I hesitated a moment, then forced myself to add, "Did you, by chance, see my bra in the laundry? I can't find it."

He turned his back to me, pulling things from the cupboards as he answered.

"I saw you didn't have much to wear and left to find you more. Groth stayed. You were safe. I took your clothes with me to compare sizes. I found more but lost your bra. The new clothes are in the bathroom if you want to shower while I make breakfast."

When he'd admitted to opening the door last night because he'd been worried that I'd left, I hadn't known what to think. But hearing that he'd gone out in the middle of the night, which we'd already established was dangerous, just to get me more to wear? His thoughtfulness gently pierced my heart. Yes, losing the bra sucked, but outer clothes were so much more important.

"That was really nice of you to do that for me, Azio. Don't worry about the bra. I'm sure I'll be able to find another one."

He grunted, and eager to see what he'd found, I left him in the kitchen.

A small stack of clothes waited in the bathroom. Underwear, as promised, shirts, and shorts. The items were far from the sturdier clothes I'd been imagining. I picked up the vivid pink thong and chewed on my lip. A thong was at the bottom of the list for preferred undergarments, but beggars couldn't be too choosy. Clean was clean.

The shorts were a little abrupt for my taste, too, and the shirts could barely be called shirts. Made out of threadbare material, they wouldn't preserve any modesty. Especially without a bra. It would be like wearing nothing at all.

I felt so bad that there wasn't anything in the pile I wanted to wear and wondered how offended Azio would be if I reappeared in the same clothes I'd worn to bed. Maybe I could get away with wearing the shorts with yesterday's shirt.

Hoping that the compromise would be enough to prevent any possible ripples in our tenuous cohabitation, I stripped and got to showering. Maybe there were some thong wearers in town who'd be willing to trade for a regular set of briefs. I didn't need sexy. I needed sturdy.

Wait. Did I?

I'd already acknowledged that I didn't have the same responsibilities here. In fact, I'd spent the entire prior day watching movies. Not exactly a strenuous activity. And a thong would work in my benefit if or when I finally made up my mind about having a baby.

I rinsed my hair and imagined propositioning Azio while wearing nothing but a thong. Every scenario that I ran through my head ended with me terrified and close to passing out. That made-up terror bled over into reality so much that I had to turn off the water, brace my hands on my knees, and give up that line of thinking.

Disappointment bit into me as I dried off and acknowledged I wouldn't be pregnant any time soon.

Moving on autopilot, I bent for the clothes I'd removed. They weren't on the floor. Confused, I looked at the closed toilet seat then the counter where the new clothes waited.

"What in the hell…"

My clothes, my safe underwear, were gone.

I reluctantly reached for the thong. However, the moment that string penetrated my crack, I shook my head and hurried to tug them off.

"Nope. Not happening."

Leaving the rejected thong on the floor, I snatched up a pair of shorts. The bottom half of my butt cheeks hung out when I checked the mirror. It wasn't awful, though. Between that and the exposed curve of my lower back, I felt kind of sexy.

The addition of a see-through t-shirt did nothing to make the outfit more respectable. There was no way I could walk out the door in this.

"Azio?" I called.

"Yes, Terri," he immediately answered from the other side of the door.

I frowned and suspicion flooded me.

"Why are you in the hallway?"

"To see if you like the clothes I found you?" He said it like a question. As if he wasn't sure why he was in the hall, which only made my suspicions climb as I looked down at my clearly visible nipples.

"Did you lose my bra on purpose?" I asked.

Silence answered my question, and my stomach churned with worry. He'd gotten rid of my bra and gifted me hoochie clothes. Why? The answer to that seemed pretty obvious, and my thoughts turned to how I'd just been thinking of sex and babies...and how badly those thoughts had ended.

I wasn't ready.

Suddenly, I wasn't sure if I would ever be ready to have a baby with one of the fey.

But I didn't have anywhere else to go.

"Am I still safe here?" I asked.

"Yes, Terri. You are safe."

"Why did you take my clothes?"

"To wash them."

"So I'll get them back?"

There was a beat of silence before he answered, "Yes, Terri."

"I'm very grateful that you went out to get me more clothes, but I'm feeling very exposed in this kind of shirt. Is there any chance I could wear the one that's on the dryer?"

"I lost that one."

"I just saw it this morning."

There was a longer length of silence.

"I'm trying not to feel afraid, but I don't understand why you're taking my clothes away and leaving me with very little. I mean...I think I do understand, and that's why I'm starting to feel afraid." I twisted my hands in front of me. "I don't want to be forced to have sex yet. Can I please have some more time?"

Something thumped outside the door, and I jumped.

"I'm sorry. I promise I'm trying. I just—"

My vision tunneled, and I gripped the counter as my knees buckled.

Nothingness swallowed me whole.

It never took me long to come back from a faint. Five minutes was the longest, and that had been in high school. Usually, once I started coming to, I wasn't disoriented.

This time, though, I felt myself moving sideways, and that screwed with my head in a big way. I remembered the bathroom and the clothes and freaking out that Azio was preparing me for a good time—his good time—and then fainting. My movement should be downward or still.

I opened my eyes and looked up at Azio.

He wasn't looking at my head, though. He was staring at my chest. Dazed and confused, I followed the direction of his attention and saw my nipples. Seeing them made me aware of the air caressing half my ass.

A small sound escaped me. Part fear. Part gasp for air. And my gaze jerked back up to Azio, and the blatant hunger in his eyes.

He slowly met my gaze. The hunger disappeared, replaced by...nothing.

My pulse fluttered wildly, and I knew I needed to calm down and ask some questions. Like why he was carrying me and what he meant to do, but I didn't get the chance before he stopped walking and leaned forward. The moment my back hit the mattress, my eyes went wide.

A choked sound wheezed from my throat.

"You are safe," he said.

"She does not believe you. You are scaring her."

I shifted my attention to the other fey at the foot of my

bed. While his words sounded like he was ready to be my hero, he was staring at my very visible chest just as hungrily as Azio.

Two fey.

First, they took my clothes.

Then, they carried me to bed.

Together.

My vision started to tunnel. I opened my mouth to scream but nothing came out.

THE SOUND of worried voices greeted me as I slowly swam back to consciousness. Again.

"We keep scaring her," a male voice said.

"Uh, the Terri I know wouldn't dress to show her tits to the world," a familiar voice replied. "No, shit you scared her if you took her clothes and left that for her to wear. What were you thinking?"

While I recognized Brooke's voice, I didn't recognize the man who answered.

"They wanted to see her breasts."

"They move more without the bra," the first male, Azio, said. "Ghua said that breasts have tips called nipples and nipples are sensitive and pucker when they are ready to be licked or sucked. I only wanted to see them so I would know when she is ready for my mouth."

I remembered Azio and Groth, but everything was still swimmy and not making sense. Why were they talking about licking nipples?

Brooke let out a frustrated groan.

"Out. All of you. I'll sit with her until she wakes up."

"But—"

"Out, before I nut all of you."

There was a shuffle of noise and then silence.

Brooke sighed and took my hand in hers. I waited a moment with my eyes closed and let everything come back to me. Once it did, I winced at my stupidity.

Passing out twice in a row broke all the rules. And staying out long enough for Brooke to get here? Well, it was a damn miracle I was still alive. Anything could have happened. Raped by two fey would have been the least of my worries if there'd been another infected breech.

"Is that wince because you hurt something or because they're making your brain hurt?"

I opened my eyes and looked at her.

"How am I still alive when I pass out every time something scares me? My fears are going to kill me."

She nodded slowly.

"I think you might be right. Azio said you passed out in the bathroom because he switched out your clothes. He's not sure why you passed out the second time."

I slowly sat up then stood up, doing a slow turn for her.

"Yeah," she said. "I figured that was the reason for the first time."

"The second time was because I came to with two of them leering at my chest while putting me in my bed."

She made a face.

"I can see where you'd misunderstand the situation."

"Misunderstand? Everyone knows they want women. They dressed me for sex, Brooke. What's to misunderstand?"

CHAPTER TEN

"What do you want, Terri?"

Brooke's abrupt change in topic confused me, and I sat down on my barely clad bottom.

"I don't understand."

"Wayne was always a dick to you. Nothing over the top, but he was rarely sweet to you, and you always seemed unhappy. Even on the days that Bobby came back with enough food to stuff us. So, I guess I'm asking what would bring you joy.

"If all you focus on are the things that scare you, you're probably going to keep passing out. But maybe, if you have that one thing that you really want and can focus on that instead, you won't be on your back so much.

"So, what do you want out of life? Don't think about the past. Think about the present. Right now. What do you want?"

I gave her question some real consideration. The answer that always came to mind first didn't this time, though. Oh, I still wanted a baby with every fiber of my being, but I realized that would never happen because I was too afraid of all the steps I'd need to take to get there.

Essentially, I'd created my own hell loop. I wanted a baby but not to watch it die. It needed parents strong enough, brave enough, to protect it. A fey father would deliver on the strength. But every time I paid attention to their predatory eyes and remembered how easily they killed, I froze up on the inside. I would never have what I truly wanted until I figured out how to be completely fine around the fey.

"I don't want to be afraid anymore."

"Yeah, I know. That's what we're trying to work on."

I shook my head. "No, I mean of the fey. Ultimately, they're going to be what bring me joy." As I said it, I flushed, which Brooke noted with a growing grin.

"And, boy, can they. Okay. Good for you. We're going to help you reach out and take what you want. Now, what exactly are you afraid of?"

"Their enormous size and strength and ability to rip someone's head off without seeming to exert even a little effort." I made a face and added, "And their eyes. They remind me of this barn cat my grandparents had. That thing was mean as hell and killed every single bird my grandma unintentionally baited in with her birdfeeder. That cat hissed if you even looked at it. It ripped me up when I was seven for trying to chase it away from the birds. I can still remember the way its pupils narrowed to slits."

I shuddered, and Brooke gave me a sympathetic look.

"First, there are a few things you should know about these guys. They aren't aggressive toward women. At all. Ever. Yeah, they might look longingly at you, but Mya's been super strict about consent. Like, they wouldn't touch any of your fun bits even if you landed on their face."

She laughed at the disbelief in my expression.

"I swear. It's true. They might steal your clothes and look until their eyes fall out, but they won't touch unless they are verbally invited to do so. Or unless you're in danger. They'll touch you then, too, but only platonically and only to keep you safe. That's why Azio brought you to your bed, by the way. He heard you through the door and got to you before you hit your head on anything."

I wasn't buying it, and she knew it based on her grin.

"I see that you still doubt me. That's fine. But I'll trade you three pot roasts in my freezer for three tests—your choice of what kind—to prove that I'm right."

"My choice?"

"Yep. Do something you think will upset them. Outcome doesn't matter. You get the roast just for testing them."

I snorted. "If I do something I think will upset them, I promise you the outcome very much matters."

"I'll be here to protect you."

"So we can both die?"

"Pfft. So little faith. Come on. What's something that would have really upset Wayne?"

"Not pulling my weight. Taking more than my share of food. Telling him I didn't want to have sex. Not having dinner done on time. Making him look bad in front of his friends." I opened my mouth to keep going but she held up her hand.

"I think that gives us a few options. Come on." She stood and headed for the door.

"Wait. My shirt."

However, my protest came too late.

She swung the door open and stopped short at the sight of the three fey she'd revealed in the hallway. They all wore wary expressions as their gazes flicked from her to me then back again.

"When I said to get out, I meant go away. Lingering outside the door to listen to everything we say isn't nice."

Solin, her fey, tugged at his ear and gave her a sheepish look.

"I'm sorry, my Brooke. I did not know."

"I know, baby."

She looked at Azio and held out her hand. "Your shirt. Now."

He immediately took it off and gave it to her. She looked back at me with a sly wink and tossed it my way.

"There you go. A better shirt to wear."

She faced Azio and Groth again as I held the material to my chest.

"You two are going to play a game with Terri. It's called Terri Says. The rules are simple. If you want her to stay here, living with you, you do everything she says. Want to play?"

They both glanced at me, their pupils narrowing, and nodded.

"Alrighty, then." She pivoted to look at me. "You're up."

A flush crept into my cheeks as I glanced from her to the fey.

"Can you turn around?" I asked them.

They grunted and immediately gave me their backs. I hurriedly tugged Azio's still warm shirt over my head, Brooke was grinning at me the whole time.

"Come on. Let's have some fun."

She led the way out of the room and down to the kitchen.

"Solin, how would you feel if I asked you to make me a plate of eggs and rub my feet while I ate?" she asked.

"I would feel your toes first. Then your ankle. Can I use my mouth?"

The complete turnaround in conversation made me stumble, and I almost fell down the stairs. Only Azio's quick reflexes, and the banded arm he whipped around me, prevented it. I clutched at the anchor as my heart pounded.

Brooke glanced back at me, her gaze dipping to Azio's forearm just below my breasts.

"Nice save, Azio," she said, giving me a significant look.

It had been. And even though my heart was trying to beat its way out of my throat, it wasn't because of fey-fear. Just normal falling to my death fear. I let out a shaky breath and uncurled my fingers from his large bicep.

"Thank you, Azio," I said.

He grunted and slowly withdrew his hold, probably not trusting that I wouldn't fall on my face. I couldn't blame him.

In the last few days I'd been far from my steady, fairly graceful self. But really, who could blame me for the almost fall just now? Brooke's comment about a foot rub while she ate breakfast would have probably had any human man rolling his eyes and saying, "yeah, right." Not Solin, though. He hadn't only not minded, but he'd been very into the suggestion.

When we reached the bottom of the stairs, I glanced back at Brooke's fey. Sure enough. It was easy to see the bulge in the front of his pants. He'd really liked the idea of playing with her feet.

While the three fey went to the kitchen, Brook led me to the living room.

"Do they have foot fetishes?" I asked softly.

She laughed and shook her head.

"They have female fetishes. They want to know everything about us. Watch us. Touch us."

She wasn't helping my nerves and knew it. Shaking her head at me, she nudged me to take a seat.

"Relax. Try to have fun. No one is going to die."

She'd seen the same violent endings I had, but didn't have an ounce of fear for them. Why not?

The answer came with a plate of food. Solin handed it to her and immediately sat on the floor, tugging off her socks while she dug into her helping of eggs.

She moaned in appreciation when he started rubbing her feet.

"Did you know that they're learning how to give massages? Whoever decided to teach them that was the smartest person ever," Brooke said as Groth handed me a plate.

"Can I rub your feet?" he asked hopefully.

"Yes, you may," Brooke said when I didn't immediately answer.

Groth shook his head slowly.

"That is not Terri's consent. She needs to say it."

"Uh, I'd rather not," I said, my pulse already starting to pick up pace with my worry.

His shoulders slumped a little, and he moved off to the side, taking a seat where he could stare at me.

I glanced at Azio, who stood off to the side, watching me just as intently. When he caught my gaze, he nodded at me.

"Eat, Terri. You are safe."

I realized then he wasn't only telling me I was safe from the infected and hellhounds in his presence. I was also safe from him. From both of them.

Ducking my head, I ate the breakfast he'd made for me and savored each bite. The eggs were delicious, made even better by the fact he'd cooked them just for me.

As soon as we were finished, Brooke arched a brow at me.

"You're up."

"Actually, I think I'm good for now."

"You sure you don't want a few roasts for your freezer?"

"You've proven your point. I'm less worried than I was before. Maybe."

"You're not really selling the confidence here."

"I know. I just don't think I'm ready to push at boundaries yet."

"Fair enough. Want to do breakfast together again tomorrow?"

Solin started to chuckle.

"Brooke does not like to cook," he confided, flashing his teeth at me. They were pointed. Like that damn barn cat.

Brooke dug an elbow into my side when his smile started to fade.

"Cut it out, Terri. Do you know how much talking and other things I had to do to convince him he has an amazing smile? They've changed so much already because of our petty fears. They wear clothes that are too small and uncomfortable just to look more human. They don't smile.

They lose sleep to keep us safe. They gave up their homes. They—"

"I'm sorry," I said, holding up my hands. "Solin, you do have a lovely smile. My surprise doesn't mean anything other than you're the first one I've seen do it."

Brooke made a harrumphing sound as she stood and wrapped her arms around his waist.

"Come on, baby. Let's go home so I can make you smile some more."

He picked her up and strode to the door.

"I really am sorry," I said, quickly standing and hurrying after the pair.

He handed her her shoes, and she waved away my concern.

"It's fine. You can make it up to me by cooking something good for breakfast. See you then!"

And then I was alone with my fey.

CHAPTER ELEVEN

My fey. The phrase echoed around in my head throughout the rest of the day as we watched movies, and they took turns making me food or bringing me something to drink. They were infallibly considerate.

I even caved on the foot massage once I had lounge pants on again. Azio rubbed my right foot while Groth claimed my left. They were both gentle and watched my reactions more than the movie playing. Of course I enjoyed being pampered. Who wouldn't? They were attentive to my needs. And through a hundred small actions, they let me know they were both very interested in any scrap of attention I would willingly give them.

However, that concentrated level of attention left me feeling a bit overwhelmed and concerned. Especially when I caught a glimpse of hunger in their gazes.

Even though neither touched me without permission, I went to bed that night with the door firmly closed and a request that they leave it that way unless there was an emergency. To my relief, it was still shut in the morning, and all my clothes were exactly where I'd left them.

Rather than shower, I went downstairs to start breakfast for Solin and Brooke's visit. Thanks to the powdered eggs and a surplus of baking ingredients, I put together a savory hash brown breakfast casserole.

Groth and Azio watched me move around the kitchen and asked a million questions again. I didn't mind the questions. Cooking curiosity I could handle. Yesterday's subtle female curiosity had been a little unnerving, though. Which is why I was anxious for Brooke's visit. She'd known exactly how they would behave and had been right about the boundaries they held to.

I was hoping she would be able to give me more insight this morning. Like what my long-term role would be here... with two fey.

Once the casserole was in the oven, I excused myself to get ready and asked them both to respect my privacy and stay out of the bathroom while I was using it. Like the day before, they quickly agreed to my request.

By the time I emerged, I could hear Brooke's voice downstairs and hurried to join her.

She was all smiles when she saw me and motioned for me to join her on the couch and let the fey serve us. While they were busy plating our food, I took a calming breath and quietly asked my first question.

"What exactly is going on here?"

"What do you mean?"

"Are they both interested in me?"

"Probably."

"So they want to share me?"

Something dropped in the kitchen. When I glanced to see what, I found all three fey frozen and staring off in different directions.

"They're acting weirder than normal, right?" I asked softly.

Brooke laughed.

"They are. But ignore them for a moment. Do you want Groth and Azio to share you?"

"I'm not even sure I can handle one fey, never mind two."

"And when you say handle...?"

"Be in a physically intimate relationship."

"Sex," she said bluntly. "You're not sure if you can have sex with two at once, or are you not sure you can juggle two sexually active relationships simultaneously?"

I stared at her for a long moment.

"Are you purposely trying to see what it takes to shock me?"

"Nope. I'm spelling it out so those poor, freaking out fey in the kitchen can decide if they want to try fainting or not."

I glanced at the still frozen fey. All of their ears were a deep, dark grey, almost to the point of being black. Something eased inside of me, seeing that I'd unintentionally made them so uncomfortable. Their disconcertion made them so human.

"I'm not trying to freak anyone out," I said. "I'm just trying to understand what they expect of me."

"Well, I'm pretty sure they were hoping you'd pick one of them to be your happily-ever-after man. But now that you mentioned two, they're probably quietly deciding if they can share you. And that's why I spelled out the sharing option. I'm not sure threesomes are something they'd enjoy. I mean, Solin doesn't mind his brothers knowing the details of our sexcapades, but he's not keen on me walking around town naked for everyone to see. They're a little possessive but not in a smothering way."

My face couldn't be any hotter. Or redder. The idea of a threesome with Groth and Azio wasn't something I wanted to try. Ever.

"No threesome. That's not what I was saying."

"Okay. So taking turns having sex then? My hat's off to you, Terri. I want to sit on an icepack this morning, and that's only with one fey. I couldn't imagine trying to keep up with two of them."

My heart was starting to race. But, thankfully, the fey were still locked in place, which prevented me from having a complete freak-out.

"I'm not interested in sleeping around," I said, my voice a little choked. "One man is more than enough."

And just like that, the tension in the kitchen eased, and they started moving.

Brooke grinned at me. While she didn't say it, her expression screamed, "I told you so."

"You hold their fates in your very capable hands. They're trying to impress you and hope you'll choose one of them. But if you don't choose either of them, they won't be upset. They'd be happy if you chose any of the fey."

Azio and Solin came forward with our plates. Both of their faces were still dark with their blushes.

"Thank you," I said quietly and accepted my portion from Azio.

"Thanks, babe," Brooke said.

Solin frowned at her. "You should have told me your pussy was too sore for my kisses this morning. I would have been more gentle."

I made a choked noise, which made her grin as she answered.

"My pussy is never too sore for your kisses. But I might need to let you draw me in the bath again today."

He grunted and folded into a sitting position at her feet, which she happily surrendered to his ministrations. While she basked in his attention, my stomach tightened, and I slowly took a bite of my food as I considered what she'd revealed.

The fey liked sex. A lot of it and often based on that little exchange. Sex wasn't my thing. It wasn't awful, or at least it hadn't been with Wayne. But it wasn't something I'd beg for at any point. It had been more enjoyable when I'd known there might be a baby because of it and had gotten less so once that possibility was gone.

My gaze shifted to Groth, the bigger of the two, then Azio. They both studied me closely.

I didn't want to make either of them think I was being a tease, but I wasn't sure how a long-term relationship would work with either of them. Groth's size had made him extra worrisome *before* I knew about their libidos. But maybe I needed to reconsider offering myself up to Azio, now, too.

"You got pretty quiet," Brooke commented. "What's on your mind?"

"Nothing I want to ask you."

She laughed. "It's so much better to be frankly open around them. Trust me. I learned that the hard way."

She'd been right about so much so far, so I squared my shoulders and asked what needed asking.

"How many times a day do you two have sex?"

"I managed four actual intercourse sessions yesterday and one very careful oral. I'm hoping I build up callouses or something, though, because Solin would like to play with my bits twenty-four-seven."

"Not if it hurts you," he said.

She leaned forward and gave him a chaste kiss.

"And that's why I love you." She turned to me. "Why are you asking?"

"Because I'm not really a fan of sex. Three times a week, I could manage. Four times a day? I'm not sure I'm fey material if that's their typical sex drive."

I looked at Groth then Azio. "I'm sorry. I didn't mean to mislead you."

"We are happy you chose to live here. You do not need to choose any of us. We will still care for you," Groth said.

I gave him a grateful smile that slowly died at Azio's next words.

"Perhaps you only dislike human sex. Maybe you would like fey sex."

One look at my wide eyes and Brooke's laughter filled the room. Azio's lips twitched, assuring me that my shock had amused him as well.

"It is something to consider," he said with a slight shrug.

I hesitantly nodded, not that I actually thought sex with a fey would be better than with a human guy. If anything, it sounded worse. Sex until sore? No, thank you.

After we finished our breakfast, Solin produced two decks of cards, and we played War in pairs with a rotating observer. An hour slipped by without my notice and then another. When Brooke stood with a stretch and went off to use the bathroom, I noticed the way Solin stared after her, as if watching her leave was tearing him apart on some level.

It probably was. Brooke had started seeing him a little more than a week ago. Not nearly enough time for the mindless infatuation phase to wear off. Especially if they were going at it like bunnies.

When she returned, he stood and met her halfway.

"Are you still sore, my Brooke?"

A slow smile parted her lips.

"Only a little. Feel like going home and sketching something?"

His answer was to pick her up and start for the door.

"I guess I'll see you tomorrow morning," she called before it closed behind them.

I sighed without realizing how it would sound to Groth and Azio.

"Would you like to play more War?" Groth asked.

"I could make you popcorn," Azio offered.

Another day of movies and popcorn would be a safe, if slightly uncomfortable, way to pass the time. But that wouldn't help any of us. Thanks to Brooke's very embarrassing clarifications this morning, I knew both my fey housemates were open to having a relationship with me. And if I ever wanted a baby, I needed to figure out how to be okay with being with a fey.

I glanced at Azio then Groth. They watched me closely, their eyes doing that thing they did. I wanted to shiver. Instead, I forced myself to take a mental step toward my goal.

"I don't think popcorn or games are what I need."

"Tell us what you need. We will get it for you," Groth said, stepping closer.

Azio's gaze reflected the same earnest desire to do whatever it took to keep me here, and it helped bolster my determination.

"My fainting has stopped me from leaving Tenacity for supplies. I don't want to be useless. I'd like to try to do my part if you think I won't be too much of a liability."

"You are not useless," Azio said firmly.

"Right now, I feel that way, though. Would I put you in danger if we went outside the wall together to look for food?"

"No, we would not be in danger," Azio said. "There is no need for you to leave for supplies, though. We can find whatever you want."

"I know. But I think I need to do this. Please."

Azio and Groth shared a look.

"It's not safe with only two of us," Groth said. "We would need to ask for volunteers to help."

"How many?" I asked.

"Five more," Azio said.

They both watched me, waiting for my decision and likely thinking the same thing weighing on my mind. I'd passed out the last time I'd been surrounded by fey. How was this time going to be any better?

"Okay," I said. "Five more. How soon can we leave?"

CHAPTER TWELVE

I DRESSED IN JEANS AND LAYERED T-SHIRTS AND DID MY BEST TO ignore the way my nerves twisted my stomach into knots. Going braless on a seven-fey expedition didn't help the cause. After a few steadying breaths, I left the room and joined Azio downstairs.

With my jacket in his hands, he waited for me by the door. I gave him a weak smile and let him help me, hoping he wouldn't notice how badly my hands were shaking.

"Your heart is racing. There is no need for you to leave," he said.

"You can hear my heart racing?"

"Yes." He moved my hair out from the collar of the jacket, and his fingers brushed against my skin in a light caress. "Please stay."

I turned to look up at him, my heart racing harder when I met his gaze.

"If I stay, nothing will change. And I really want things to change. My fears are holding me back and keeping me from the things I really want. And, no, I'm not going to tell you what I want. Not yet. Maybe someday, though. If this works."

He grunted and zipped my jacket for me.

"Will you allow me to carry you?"

"Yes. Please."

He picked me up before opening the door, which made me giggle until he opened it with only a minor adjustment in how he was holding me. The show of strength was both reassuring and fear-evoking at the same time.

I caught a brief glimpse of a group of fey waiting outside before I closed my eyes.

"Where would you like to go?" Azio asked.

"You choose."

"What would you like to find?"

"Food would be good. Maybe some clothes?"

He grunted, and I felt him start running. His movements barely jostled me. That changed when we reached the wall. My stomach flipped at his sudden jump, and I barely contained the squeal that wanted to erupt.

Then wind battered my face, and I turned my head into his chest. While the weather was still cold, it wasn't unbearable in his arms. Warmth radiated from his torso, keeping my nose and hands comfortable. My backside, though? Not so much. However, I'd known this wouldn't be some happy outing, so I didn't complain about my discomfort.

Minutes passed without any other noise but the wind and the slight rustle of their passing. I lifted my head after a while to take a quick peek. The fey ran in a circular formation around Azio. No, around *me*.

When one of them noticed my attention, he glanced my

way and nodded. I managed one in return before tucking my face into Azio's chest once more.

There was no mistaking the way he leaned down this time and brushed his cheek against the top of my head. I smiled to myself, appreciating his gesture of comfort.

If I put aside my fears about his strength and my aversion to his eyes, I really did like Azio. Groth too. But there was something sweeter about Azio. Which was kind of crazy since he was also the sterner of the two. Maybe that's what I liked most. He wasn't as much of a pushover as Groth. I grinned into his chest, thinking of how he'd plotted to lose my bra.

Azio was willing to push at my boundaries but still respected them. That was what I needed to make my dreams of a future a reality.

Eventually, the group slowed, and I looked up again. A farmhouse loomed ahead.

"This is a place we've visited in the past," Azio said. "There are no clothes or food. But it has heat and water if you want to stop."

"Yes, please."

Two of the fey ran ahead, and I watched them disappear inside.

"They're checking for infected, aren't they?"

Azio grunted.

It didn't take long for the one of the pair to reappear and wave us forward, and I couldn't have been more grateful. My butt was in desperate need of a thawing. Staying focused on that discomfort made it easier to deal with seven sets of fey eyes watching me once I was inside.

"Would you like to stand?" Azio asked.

"Please."

He put me down and let me hang onto his arm as I shook out my legs.

"Is this how many fey usually watch over a human on the supply runs?" I asked.

Azio shrugged. I released him and nonchalantly tried to rub some warmth into my backside. It didn't work too well, so I moved around, pretending to look around the house.

"How much farther until we get to where we're going?" I asked.

"We're halfway there."

"Where's there?"

"Warrensburg."

I nodded slowly, recalling what I'd heard of the place.

"Isn't that pretty picked over, foodwise?"

"We will find food and clothes."

The way he said that didn't reassure me. Sure, we might find food and clothes, but what would it take to get to them. I mentally scolded myself. That was the kind of thinking I needed to get rid of and why I was doing this. I needed to learn to trust the fey. To trust Azio.

"Are you hurt?" he asked, confusing me.

"What? No. Why?"

"You keep rubbing yourself?"

I flushed and jerked my hands away from my butt.

"Nope. Fine."

He glanced at the other fey. Two left the house, and the rest went off to look at other things.

"Will you allow me to help you?"

"You are."

He sighed and strode toward me. Before I knew what he

intended, my face was pressed to his chest, and he was grabbing my ass with both hands.

The sound that tore from me could only be described as a squawk.

"Shh. I am not hurting you. You need to warm before we leave again."

I turned my head to breathe and grabbed his waist for support.

"A little warning would have been nice."

"So you could pretend you didn't need this?"

I made a face because he was probably right. Huffing, I leaned into him. He seemed to take that as permission to start moving his hands. I opened my mouth to tell him to stop, then snapped it closed again.

Wasn't this the whole point, Terri? I thought to myself. *This is nothing compared to what you are thinking of asking him to do to you.*

So I held still and let him rub some feeling into my butt. And it wasn't horrible. He was gentle and not overly grabby.

I didn't realize how okay it was until I felt myself relaxing into his embrace. He brushed his cheek against the top of my head, letting me know he'd noticed. Maybe this wasn't a bad thing at all. He was touching me, and my heart wasn't racing. I'd take that win and carry on.

"Better?" he asked after a while.

"Yes. Thank you."

The others must have been in hearing range because they promptly rejoined us.

"Would you like Groth to carry you?" Azio asked.

I'd assumed Azio would continue carrying me, which

was a bit rude. Holding another person while running had to be exhausting.

"Sure."

Groth stepped forward and scooped me up just as gently as Azio had. It wasn't the same, though, when I had to tuck my face into his shirt. While I was grateful that I was comfortable enough with him that my heart didn't flutter with fear, I still wished Azio's arms were the ones around me.

Eventually, Groth slowed, and I heard a distant moan. My head snapped up, and I looked around wildly.

"You are safe, Terri," Groth said.

I noted we'd lost two of our seven-fey team and felt less than safe.

Azio moved closer, keeping pace with Groth.

"Do you want to stop?" he asked.

Ahead, I could see houses—the outskirts of the city.

I shook my head.

"There will be infected," he said.

"I know."

The next several minutes passed in a blur. The two fey had run ahead to gain the attention of any wandering infected. We found evidence of their passing via a trail of headless bodies in the street.

"These houses have been cleared," Azio said quietly.

I silently took his word for it, and we moved farther into the city, where there were no bodies. My skin crawled at the unnatural silence in the middle of the expansive urban sprawl. That eerie foreboding grew when the fey slowed and looked at me.

"Which house would you like to check first?" Groth asked.

My gaze swept over the surrounding homes. They all looked equally scary.

"You choose," I whispered.

They picked one at random. Two more fey went inside to clear it while Azio and another waited with us for the signal to enter.

The house wasn't a bad pick. Inside, we discovered a pantry full of food. Before I could get too excited, Azio explained we couldn't take everything. However, they would return for whatever I couldn't fit inside the backpack he'd found.

I moved around on my own two feet, looking at what the house had to offer. Two fey remained within touching distance at all times. Their nearness helped, but my nerves still felt stretched to the point of breaking.

The food helped distract from some of the fear, though. I found some chocolate chips and a pound of butter. Both went into the bag along with some clothes I thought might work. I made neat stacks of blankets, pillows, and clothes in the kitchen for them to retrieve later.

"We might not need it, but Tenacity could use all of that," I said when I finished.

Azio grunted and turned his head suddenly to look down the hallway.

Groth picked me up without asking and backed away.

"Close your eyes, Terri," Azio commanded as the access panel to the attic crawl space lifted.

With every fiber of my being, I wanted to do what he

said. But my eyes didn't close. My gaze remained glued to that dark space in the ceiling.

Pale, blue-tinted fingers appeared, gripping the edge. Then, tangled clumps of long hair dangled down. Ever so slowly, the rest of the head appeared. Decay hadn't touched the woman's face, and her brown eyes glowed with a faint hint of red.

Their eyes weren't supposed to have color. They were supposed to be milky white.

"Take her," Azio said. "Don't stop for anything."

Groth sprinted for the door as the infected woman fell into the hallway.

I clutched at him, lifting myself enough to look over his shoulder. The woman's head tilted, but her eyes remained on my retreat. Azio growled and rushed her. She opened her mouth and let out an ungodly moan that echoed in the walls.

Groth cleared the front door a moment before Azio reached her. I couldn't see what he did, but I heard the faint wet squelch. Her death came too late, though.

More calls rang out in the street around us. It didn't matter that there were three other fey with us; terror clawed at my insides. This wasn't the first time I'd heard these calls. The infected had breached the military base we'd called home several times, and each one had been worse than the one before. People died. They always died. Now, we were the only people around.

"We will keep you safe, Terri," Groth said. "Don't look. Stay awake."

Right. Fainting now would be bad. Very bad.

Yet, with the way my heart hammered against my rib

cage, I didn't see how I'd avoid it. Closing my eyes, I pressed my forehead against his chest and fisted my hands in his shirt. I tried my hardest to focus on each rise and fall of his chest, but I couldn't shut out the sounds.

Moans. Yells. Grunts. Squelches. I knew that infected were everywhere and that the fey were killing some. But Groth wasn't slowing down for any of it. He jumped suddenly. The upward jolt made my stomach clench and robbed me of breath. I kept my eyes closed, not wanting to know what was happening.

He grunted and landed hard a second later. Then repeated the grunt, jump, land process for several long minutes before stopping suddenly.

Breathing hard, he held me close to his chest. I opened my eyes and stared at my white-knuckled grip on his shirt. Neither of us moved. In the distance, I heard more moans.

Then another soft call nearby, letting me know we weren't yet out of danger.

Swallowing hard, I closed my eyes again and pressed my forehead against his chest. He shifted me slightly in his arms, holding me more securely as his breathing started to slow.

A thump nearby made me jerk in his arms.

"Shh," he said softly.

Several more thumps followed. Then we were moving again. This time when he jumped, I looked and saw we were running along the rooftops.

Two of the fey ran in front of us, their shirts gone and their pants coated with blood. I didn't try to see what the rest looked like.

It felt like it took a lifetime to reach the outskirts of

Warrensburg. When we did, the group stopped so we could listen for any nearby infected.

A howl, not a moan, echoed somewhere behind us. The sound of a hellhound was unmistakable and sent a shiver through me.

However, the fey around me seemed completely unconcerned by the fact a hellhound was awake and making itself known in the middle of the day. Or maybe that was why they watched the open area between the houses and the trees so intently.

Either way, I was positive I wouldn't make it back to Tolerance alive.

CHAPTER THIRTEEN

"Do you read, Terri?" Azio asked.

I barely heard his quiet words over the pulse thundering in my ears.

"Terri, do you read?" he asked again when I didn't answer.

"Yes," I managed. "Why?"

"There are many books in our basement. Maybe you would like to read one when we get home. Cheri told Farco she finds them relaxing."

One of the other fey snorted, and I saw him grin before he turned his head. Disbelief robbed me of some of my panic. Had Azio just made a joke about me relaxing? Now? Moments after hearing the howl?

I turned my stunned gaze on him. He, however, looked completely serious. And covered in gross bits.

"It was only an idea. Your heart was racing."

Brownish-red smeared across his cheek, and his shirt was torn.

"You lost some color. Are you feeling faint?"

I slowly nodded but couldn't manage to close my eyes.

There was a crescent of blood on his shoulder. A bite mark. He'd been bitten. That was why his shirt was torn. Torn while killing infected to keep them from chasing after me.

My heart stuttered a beat. The fey's immunity to infection was the biggest reason to choose one to father my future children. Humans died when bitten. There was no saving them. No coming back from it. I hoped a half-fey child would be just as immune.

"Thank you," I rasped.

He nodded. "I will find you a good book. Farco told me which ones to pick."

That same fey from before made a sound again. Before I could glance his way, another motioned for us.

"We should leave."

Groth grunted, jumped off the roof, and started to run across the field with the rest of the fey surrounding us. In two blinks, we made it to the trees. I turned my head into Groth's chest after that and held on for dear life.

It was quiet, though, as we put distance between Warrensburg and us. Breathing got a little easier when we reached another house Azio said was about halfway. Like last time, two went in. Unlike last time, one of the fey carried a body out, and Azio joined the search of the house. It took longer to ensure it was free of infected, but I didn't mind the extra caution since the sun was still high enough in the sky.

The heat was on inside, and the showers were running when we finally entered. Since Groth and I were clean, we gathered whatever I thought would fit the others. It wasn't a great selection.

However, I couldn't say I minded the view once the fey changed. The undersized t-shirts molded to every chiseled muscle they possessed on their upper halves, and the sweats and jogging shorts left little to the imagination downstairs.

While none of them minded my ogling glances, Azio's ears grew darker each time my gaze swung his way. And boy, did it swing. Unlike that water bottle he had strapped to his inner thigh.

It was profane.

Terrifying.

Faint-worthy for sure.

Why couldn't I stop staring?

I swallowed hard and forced my gaze away for the dozenth time but only managed a second before I was back looking at it.

It moved.

A twitch, then a stretch, the length crawling down his leg another two inches.

I dropped into a crouch, startling all the fey, and focused on breathing through my lightheadedness.

Pick the small one, I mocked at myself. *He's less terrifying. You should have checked his pants first!*

"I will wait outside," Azio said, his softly spoken words conveying his confusion and blame for my panic.

Guilt speared me.

"Wait. Give me a moment." He paused beside me, and I took a breath, then another. When my vision didn't tunnel, I looked up at him. "I'd like you to carry me the rest of the way. Please."

That thing in his too-tight pants twitched again. I couldn't *not* notice. It was eye-level. But I managed to maintain eye contact regardless of what was happening in his pants.

I wasn't trying to play favorites by asking Azio to carry me again. But I knew I shouldn't ask Groth since he'd just carried me, and I was far from comfortable with asking anyone else even though they seemed nice enough. I wasn't entirely sure I was comfortable with Azio carrying me.

Liar! I silently yelled at myself. Perversely, what I'd just witnessed only made me want him to carry me more. My feelings about his size remained unchanged. But I also found the evidence of his attraction to me downright flattering.

He offered his hand and helped me to my feet.

"Are you warm enough?"

"Yep. I'm warm." I was pretty sure my face was on fire and didn't think I'd survive if he wanted to touch my butt, too.

"Are you hungry?"

He motioned to one of the other fey who miraculously had the backpack from Warrensburg.

"I'm okay for now. I'd rather wait to eat until we get home."

Azio grunted, and the fey shouldered the bag. All of the muscles in his chest and side flexed with the motion. I turned my attention to Azio's torso, mentally comparing the two. Azio's chest was a bit narrower but far more defined under his formfitting shirt.

Realizing I was staring yet again, I focused on his face and noted how intently he was watching me.

"Will you tell me what happened back there?" I asked, hoping to distract us both.

"Yes."

He held out his arms, a signal he was ready for me. I moved closer and looped an arm around his shoulder as he picked me up.

I didn't miss the way he leaned in and brushed his temple against my cheek in the process of lifting me. It was kind of sweet, actually. All the subtle touches were little reminders that he cared about me.

Once we were outside and running, he started explaining.

"The infected are growing less stupid and better at hiding. I think the one in the house was older and knew to summon more to try to get to you. She was still weak and slow compared to us. Nothing for you to worry about."

"Will the infected be watching that area now? I heard from one of my housemates who goes on supply runs that the infected do that. They wait for us to come back."

Azio shrugged, the move jostling me more firmly against his chest as he ran.

"That's a yes, isn't it?" I asked. "Nothing we'd gathered is that important. Don't risk yourselves."

He chuckled.

"Food is very important. We will return, and we will be fine. You will stay home."

Like I ever wanted to leave again. The trip had served its purpose, though. I'd indirectly witnessed the carnage the fey could achieve and didn't pass out. Every action today had been made to keep me safe. Why should I fear that? I shouldn't. And while a little fear and doubt lingered, I knew I was one step closer.

Sighing, I turned my face into Azio's chest and lifted my hand to cover the place over his heart. It beat steadily under my palm, a reminder that he was a living, breathing person with thoughts and feelings like any other.

The trip home seemed to go faster than when we'd left. My butt appreciated it. By the time we cleared Tolerance's wall, it felt like I had more ice flowing through my backside than blood.

"Can I walk from here?" I asked as soon as he landed.

He grunted and let me down. The fey carrying the bag handed it over to Azio.

"Thank you for your help today," I said, taking a moment to look each of them in the eye.

They nodded in return, and each wandered off their own separate ways. In the growing shadows between the nearby houses, more fey moved. So many fey.

"Are you sure you want to walk?" Groth asked.

I took a calming breath and nodded, giving my two companions a small smile.

"I'm safe."

I repeated that to myself every time my nerves tweaked on the way home and forced myself to look up as much as possible and either nod or smile to passersby. It was a relief when I was finally safely inside the house once more.

"If I ever want to do that again, remind me how much I didn't like it, okay?" I said, removing my shoes.

"Did you find what you wanted?" Azio asked.

"I did. Thank you."

"I will make us something to eat," Groth said, moving away.

I watched him for a moment, feeling slightly guilty. I liked Groth. He was just as kind as Azio. After seeing Azio's size today, I would be so much wiser to change my mind and make a play for Groth instead. But—I shifted my gaze to Azio, who watched me—Groth didn't call to me. Something about Azio did.

"How is your shoulder?" I asked. "I saw you were bitten. Do you want Cassie to look at it?"

"No. It will heal."

This was my perfect opening. A reason to get him alone and talk to him. My stomach twisted anxiously. I could do this.

"Come on."

I held out my hand. His gaze swept from my face to my peace offering. He wrapped his hand in mine, taking a large breath at the contact, and waited for me to make the next move.

Trying not to tremble, I led him upstairs to the bathroom. The snick of the door closing sounded loud in the silence.

"I will heal," he said when I pointed to the toilet seat.

"I know. But I'd still like to help. You were bitten keeping me safe. Take off your shirt and let me at least disinfect it."

He grunted and sat. I collected the peroxide and gauze, then hesitated, glancing at myself in the mirror. Yes, disinfecting wasn't really paying him back in kind for what he'd done. And I wasn't sure it would send the message that I cared either since it tended to sting. I thought of the see-through shirt I wore under the blue one I was looking at.

I warred with myself for a few seconds before setting everything down and pulling the top t-shirt over my head. My nipples puckered at the lack of warmth, calling even more attention to my very visible chest through the transparent yellow top.

Azio didn't make a sound when I turned, and his gaze remained locked on my breasts as I moved toward him.

"Put your hands on my waist," I said. "It'll loosen the skin on your shoulder a little." The explanation hadn't been necessary to obtain his willingness. He'd grabbed me as soon as I'd said waist. But I gave it anyway so he'd understand I wasn't asking for a grope session.

He held still, not looking away once while I dabbed his wound and watched it bubble up.

"Does it hurt?" I asked.

"Yes," he rasped.

"I'm sorry. I really appreciate what you did, though." He didn't respond, and I took a moment to pep-talk myself.

"I can't thank you and Groth enough for taking me in and letting me stay with you. It's clear you're both hoping for something more with me. And I have to be honest. I'm hoping for something more too."

His fingers twitched on my sides, and he jerked his gaze from my breasts to look up at me, his pupils narrowing to slits.

"I've dreamed of having a family of my own since I was little. I want babies, Azio. Lots of them. I know how dangerous that would be in this world with a human man. But today proved it might not be so dangerous with a fey. I mean, look at you. You were bitten and fine. I want to know my kids would be fine too."

He nodded slowly.

"You won't always fear us. When you are ready, you can choose. No single fey would refuse you."

"I think I already know who I want to ask. But I'm worried about hurting someone else's feelings by choosing."

"Yes, many will be disappointed. But not sad. We will celebrate our brother's fortune."

"So Groth won't be mad at me when I choose you?"

Azio stood suddenly, lifting me with him and wrapping me in a hug. The hand on the back of my head steered me to his unbitten shoulder as he pressed me close.

"You please me more than you know, Terri. I will keep you safe and fed and warm. You will want for nothing. I swear to you."

His exuberance had the opposite effect on me. I started shaking.

He quickly released me and resumed his seat, eyes down on the hands he braced on his knees.

"Forgive me. I didn't mean to scare you."

"I know. It's okay. I just need a little more time."

"As much time as you need."

I'd waited so long already and didn't plan to stall more than necessary. My period was due any day. Once that started, the countdown would begin.

CHAPTER FOURTEEN

NIBBLING AT MY LIP, I FINISHED CLEANING AZIO'S SHOULDER.

"Are you sure Groth will be okay?" I asked, putting away the peroxide.

"Yes." Azio glanced at me quickly. "Do you want him to find another house?"

"What? No. I like having both of you here, honestly."

Being alone with Azio so soon after telling him what I wanted would feel like more pressure to do the deed. Besides, they'd opened their home to me. There was no way I would be okay with kicking either of them out. But what did Azio want?

"There's plenty of room here for all three of us. Right?" I asked hesitantly.

"Yes. He would like to stay. Even if you choose to be my female, he would still like to talk to you and learn."

"Learn?"

Azio stood and offered me his hand. Guilt poked at my conscience when he kept his gaze on his hand instead of making eye contact.

"You can look at me, Azio," I said, placing my hand in his. "Even when I'm afraid, you can look at me. If I can't manage that much, how will we ever be able to get to the point where we can make a baby?" I flushed at the words, but that didn't make them any less true.

His gaze swept over my face, and my face grew hotter.

"My fears won't magically disappear. I'll need to work on them. But if you can be a little patient with me, I think we can make this work."

"We will. Come, we will tell Groth and assure him he may stay."

He led me into the dark hallway, giving me little time to think about anything, including my shirt until we were downstairs and Groth's gaze locked on my chest. Under the bright kitchen light, the heat exploded in my face anew.

Oblivious, Azio continued to pull me forward. "Terri will choose me when she is ready. But, she wants you to stay here, too, brother."

Azio steered me to a stool, seating me like I weighed nothing, but boy did my chest bounce enough in the process. Azio noticed, based on the way he stared and trailed his fingers down my ribs before releasing me. Groth studied my chest just as raptly as Azio had, his ears darkening to black before he lifted his gaze to mine.

"Thank you for letting me stay."

Azio's fingers returned to my ribs, gently caressing me. He probably meant it as comfort since my heart was hammering away. But it felt more sensual than anything, especially with two sets of eyes hungrily watching me. Heat speared between my legs, and I struggled to draw a decent breath.

"It was your house first," I managed before slowly crossing my arms. "I'm sorry about the shirt."

He tilted his head at me. "Why? It is very pretty. Thank you for letting me see it on you."

Azio's fingers paused their play over the thin material.

"I scared you again," he said. "You were not ready to tell Groth."

Groth's expression fell a little.

"It's not that," I said, forcing myself to speak the truth plainly like Brooke had said. "It's a little awkward for me to let Groth see my chest after saying I wanted to make a baby with Azio. I'm struggling with how to deal with it."

Both fey blinked at me.

"We don't understand," Azio said finally. "What are you dealing with?"

His question broke through my embarrassment enough that I wondered just how different our cultures were. Then I remembered Brooke's comments about how they wore clothes they found uncomfortable solely to blend in better.

"Nudity?" I said, no longer sure. "Did you pick out this shirt for me for comfort or because it was see-through?"

"Both," Azio answered. "Neither of us has seen a female before. Mya says we can't ask to look. I thought the shirt would make us all happy."

"So nudity doesn't bother you?" I asked.

"We all wish there was more of it on the surface," Groth said.

I choked out a laugh, keeping my arms firmly in place. "Humans tend to be more modest."

"We know," Azio said with a sad expression as he

glanced at my arm-shield. "Does that mean you don't like the shirt?"

"No. It means wearing this shirt will take a little more courage than I'm used to. And it probably won't ever be something I can wear in public."

"Our brothers will be disappointed, but they will understand," Azio said.

"You seriously wouldn't mind if every fey here saw me naked?" I asked.

He gazed at me thoughtfully and slowly shook his head.

"I would not rob them of what so few females will ever give. A chance to see how different a woman is made from us is too special."

"A gift," Groth said in agreement.

It was a lot to wrap my head around. Oh, I wasn't about to get up and run around outside in my shirt. And I still wanted a bra. But maybe the glimpse I'd given Groth didn't need to be as big of a deal as my brain was trying to make it out to be.

"Okay. A gift. But no more sitting me in front of other people when I'm exposed in any way," I said to Azio. "Who sees me needs to be my choice."

He grunted in agreement.

"Thank you for letting me see you," Groth said. "Are all female's nipples the same size as yours? I know breast sizes are different. Angel told me. But what about nipples?"

He slid a plate in front of me and waited for an answer with an openly curious expression.

Despite beheading infected without a second thought, the fey were nothing but kind, slightly naïve grown men. It wasn't easy to wrap my head around that.

"They're like breasts," I forced myself to say. "They come in all sizes and colors, neither of which play into how they function."

Azio frowned. "Function?"

"Yes. Once a baby is born, breasts fill with milk, and the baby suckles on the nipple to draw the milk out. It's the delivery system. We call it nursing when we feed babies with our bodies." I felt like I was completely botching the explanation, but I desperately wanted the conversation to be over.

"No one told us that. Ghua said Eden likes when he sucks her nipples, and her pussy clenches around his cock when he pinches them. But not too hard. If he's too rough, Eden gets angry, and then he can't lick her pussy after she comes."

My mouth dropped open, and my gaze darted from Groth, who'd delivered that doozy of a fact, to Azio, who watched me with concern.

"I will not pinch your nipple," Azio promised. "But could I still try sucking on them even if they are meant for a baby?"

I lifted both hands to cut off this topic. However, accidentally re-exposing my boobs had the opposite effect. Their gazes dipped. Groth looked confused. Azio looked wistful.

"Is that why females like their nipples sucked?" Groth asked. "Because they want babies?"

I quickly crossed my arms again. "This conversation is making me really uncomfortable. I kind of want to skip eating and go hide in my room for a while."

"Why?" Azio asked. "I would gladly talk to you about my cock. It has two functions. Urination and—"

"I really don't want to talk about that either."

Azio sighed but didn't look away from me.

"I can hear your pulse racing. What do you fear?"

I looked down at the countertop, not to hide but to seriously consider the question because he was right. My heart was hammering away like I was one more awkward topic away from a panic attack. Why?

"I don't know," I said finally and looked up at him. "When I stopped to think about it, there's not really anything to fear. The topics are a little embarrassing, but we're just talking. I know your questions aren't meant to push me in any way. That you're only curious about our biology. Yet, I'm still struggling to be open about information that's common knowledge to us."

"You are no different from many of the other females," Groth said. "They do not like answering our questions either. Mom will if Dad is done. Angel will always answer questions, but Shax gets impatient to touch her and sends us away too soon. The rest turn pretty shades of pink like you. Mya scolds us."

Well, that just made me feel bad for them and helped kill some of my fear.

"Okay. You win. What do you want to talk about?" And to prove I was willing, I uncrossed my arms and reached for my spoon.

It was the weirdest, most awkward meal in the history of meals. And the conversation remained firmly stuck on female breasts. The differences in how a baby suckles versus a man. When a mother's milk comes in. How breasts change. How to make them feel better when they hurt.

By the time I begged for a break, I felt like they'd learned enough to award them with some kind of boob expert certificate. But they were both so grateful for my willingness to share what I knew that I couldn't let myself dwell on how uncomfortable I'd been.

"Thank you, Terri. This will help me when I have a female of my own."

"No problem, Groth."

I moved to grab my dishes, but he insisted on cleaning up.

"I think I'm going to turn in," I said. "Thank you for today."

Azio followed me to the stairs.

"Terri, will you consider changing rooms?"

"Do you want my room?"

"No. I want you to try sleeping next to me tonight."

"Why?"

"If you choose me, you would sleep next to me every night. This will be a good test to see if you like it."

What he said made complete sense, especially given the timeline I'd set for myself. Yet, I wasn't stupid. He wanted me in the same bed with him for a reason.

"Just sleep? No touching or anything else, right?" I asked.

"No touching or anything else. I swear."

"Okay. We can try it."

"Good night, Groth," I called, heading up the stairs.

"Sleep well, Terri."

I went to my room and quickly changed into a pair of

shorts before joining Azio in his room. He paused his restless pacing when I entered. The tight sweat pants didn't hide an inch of how much he was anticipating sleeping with me.

His gaze swept over my legs and lingered on my breasts. His length twitched.

"Will you tell me when I may touch you?" he asked, meeting my gaze.

"You'll be the first one to know when I'm ready."

He grunted and pulled back the covers for me.

After so much shock and awe today, crawling into Azio's bed while he ogled my butt didn't seem so out of place. He turned out the lights then I felt him get in on the other side.

"You can touch me whenever you want," he said in the dark. "You have my consent to do anything."

I laughed. "Thanks."

"Females never ask about our bodies. Why aren't you curious?"

"I've been married before, Azio. You don't have anything that's so different from Wayne. I mean, your ears and eyes are a little different, but other than that, you're the same."

He was quiet for a long moment.

"We are not the same. He told you he didn't want you. I will never be so stupid."

"That's really sweet of you, Azio. Thank you."

"Can I ask you more questions?"

"Of course."

"You said you wanted a family since you were little but had a husband. Why don't you have a baby already?"

"Wayne didn't want babies. He had a surgery to prevent it."

"Stupid," Azio said softly. "I really want to touch you, Terri. I won't, but I think about it all the time."

His honesty pierced my heart.

CHAPTER FIFTEEN

"I'M AFRAID TO SAY YES. I KNOW TOUCHING LEADS TO OTHER things."

"What things?"

"Sex."

"All of my brothers who have found females say there is nothing more pleasing than the feel of their female's pussy clenching around their cocks. I hope to feel that someday too. But not tonight. I know you need more time. I only want to hold you in my arms while I sleep and wake up with you still there."

My heart gave a lurch at his sweetness. When he'd said touch, I'd thought he'd meant petting.

"You should have said you wanted to hold me," I said, moving closer and setting my head on his shoulder. "Touching and holding are two different things."

"May I hold you?"

"Yes."

He wrapped his arms around me and nuzzled the back of my head, neck, and shoulder, inhaling deeply as he moved. My skin prickled, and I shivered at the sensation. It reminded me of way back in the day when sex had briefly been enjoyable.

"You smell good," he murmured, continuing to nuzzle and inhale.

He moved us more until we were spooning, and I did my best to ignore the erection pressing against my backside. His hand smoothed down my arm and back up again. But nothing he did felt like he was trying to start something. He truly was reveling in the simple act of holding me.

"We don't know each other well, Azio. That's going to lead to more misunderstandings in the future unless we can figure out a way to be more open and honest with each other." I took his hand in mine, gently tracing the fingers as he held still for me. "I think my previous marriage failed because we didn't respect each other's thoughts and feelings."

"Explain," he said. It wasn't commanding exactly, but the firmness in the word made me smile.

"For example, when Wayne would approach me for sex and I would tell him I wasn't interested, he would become angry and say things to try to make me feel guilty about the refusal instead of trying to understand why I was refusing."

"I promise to always ask why and try to help resolve whatever is preventing me from sinking my cock into your pussy."

I froze, and his low chuckle rumbled behind me.

"Too open and honest?" Humor laced his words.

I knew hiding from what he was really thinking wouldn't help either of us, but I needed to be honest too.

"Yes, that was startlingly open and honest. But if that's

what you're really thinking, then I wanted to hear it. Closing down or doing things that might make you feel like I'm not interested in hearing what you have to say will only frustrate you."

"I will always be interested in hearing what you have to say, and I will not be angry if you do not want sex with me. I like holding you too."

He was racking up some serious sweetness points here.

I relaxed and started playing with his fingers again.

"I'm glad. I like this too. But you weren't kidding about the helping me want sex part, were you?"

"No." He brushed his lips against my shoulder.

"Okay. You already know that I'm not that interested in sex, in general, right? I'll do whatever it takes to have a family, but I'm not sure I'll ever be the type to do it for fun again."

He turned his hand and started exploring my fingers in return.

"Again? Did you have sex for fun at one time?"

"A very long time ago."

"What changed?"

I thought back, trying to pinpoint exactly what happened.

"I think the spark just faded for both of us. In the beginning, it was new and exciting. I loved when he touched me and said sweet things. But the sweet things and the touches became less frequent. I was supposed to be turned on just because he was ready, and I'm not wired like that. He started to get frustrated. I started to feel bad about myself, which made me resentful. It snowballed from there. And after he had the surgery? Well, I didn't see any point in the act at all anymore. I typically just gave in to keep the peace."

"Thank you for telling me," Azio said. "Now, sleep. I will ask more questions in the morning."

He gently trailed his fingers over my hand then shifted his touch to my arm. The light strokes soothed me to sleep.

I moved a few times in my sleep, waking just enough to shift my position before sinking back into Azio's comforting embrace. It was easy to miss the way dawn's light crept into the room. It wasn't easy to miss the sudden gush between my legs.

Instantly awake, my eyes flew open, and I had an up-close view of Azio's neck.

"I need to go to the bathroom," I said, not moving.

He grunted, lifted his arm, and removed the calf he'd hooked around my legs.

I didn't get out of bed like a normal person. I log-rolled to the side and stood, keeping my legs tightly pinched together the entire time. Then, I walked from the knees down.

Azio said nothing behind me. I hoped that meant he had his eyes closed through the entire process.

Once I was alone in the bathroom, I confirmed what I already knew. Red rover had come over with a vengeance, which wasn't too much of a surprise.

My periods were never kind to me. Three days of heavy flow and cramping with a side of boob aches, followed by three days of moderate flow. And as if that weren't enough, I also enjoyed hair-trigger crying at stupid commercials and junk food cravings. However, it wasn't all bad. It was also the one time I was actually horny—something Wayne had never wanted to take advantage of.

The typical disgruntlement and bad mood that came with my period wasn't part of the package this time, though. I was elated. This was exactly what I'd been waiting for—the reset for the fertility countdown. I grinned as I did my best to clean myself up.

A knock on the bathroom door sent me into a panic.

"Are you okay, Terri? I smell blood."

"Smell? You can smell this?"

"Are you hurt?"

"No. I'm fine."

I reached for more toilet paper and paused when I realized cleaning up wasn't the real problem. This was a house with two single guys in it, and I needed pads. Tampons. Something more than a wad of toilet paper.

"Actually, I have a non-life-threatening problem," I said. "You wouldn't happen to have anything on hand for a period, would you?"

"I know what you need," Azio said in a rush. "Do not move. I will return quickly."

I shook my head and looked around the bathroom. Where exactly did he think I was going to go? And more importantly, did he even know what a period was? I hoped so. Rather than wait on the toilet, I stripped and used the shower to wash up.

The heat usually helped with cramps, which hadn't yet reared their ugly head.

As I enjoyed a leisurely soak, my mind wandered. In just six days, Azio and I should start having sex. My stomach gave a twist at the thought. Was I even ready? For a baby, yes. But for jumping into a relationship with another guy? I thought of Wayne and wondered if he was regretting his decision. What if he wanted to take it back and was trying to figure out a way to talk to me? That made me pause. Did I want to go back?

I'd meant every word of what I'd said last night to Azio. Wayne and I had drifted apart, but in ways I'd been too blind to see until now. We weren't nice to each other anymore. Nothing over the top cruel, but we treated strangers better than we treated each other. Abrupt words. Little digs to make each other feel bad. Was that what I really wanted for the rest of my life? No.

Even if Wayne wanted me back, I wouldn't go. But that didn't mean I was ready to jump into something new.

I stuck my face in the shower and tried to be introspective about the choices I planned to make. Was it wise to rush into having a baby with Azio? Initially, I'd thought moving faster would secure my living arrangements. That was no longer the case. Azio and Groth had made my welcome abundantly clear. Why rush then? Why not wait a few months?

The infected were scary. And getting supplies would only be scarier.

Another knock on the door made me jump.

"I have some supplies for you. Can I come in and put them on the counter?"

"Yes, please."

The door opened. "I have more downstairs. Come down when you're ready," he said.

"I will. Thank you, Azio."

The door closed again, and I turned off the water to see

what he'd found. My jaw dropped when I opened the curtain. The typical box of pads waited, along with slippers, sweat pants, normal underwear, a non-see-through shirt, and a mini bag of potato chips.

A slow smile tugged at my lips, and I started dressing in the most comfortable period clothes ever. I didn't eat the chips, though. Not yet. The snack cravings usually hit in the afternoon.

With my chips in hand, I went downstairs. Groth was in the kitchen, mixing something in a bowl, and Azio was layering the couch in blankets.

"I have a hot water bottle ready for you," he said when he saw me. "And some man-books."

"The cookie dough is almost ready," Groth said from the kitchen.

"Uh, what's going on?"

Azio returned my puzzled look.

"You have your period." He gestured to the couch. "You can relax with a hot water bottle on your stomach while you read. We have snacks and chocolate and cookie dough but can get you whatever else you want."

"You want to pamper me because I have my period?" That couldn't be right. No man ever gave a crap about the shedding of a uterine lining, no matter how miserable it made me.

"Yes," Azio said simply, and Groth echoed his sentiment.

The first light twinge of a cramp encouraged me to grab this gift with both hands.

"Okay. Pamper away."

I let Azio fuss over the pillows behind me and tuck the blanket around my legs. When he set his large hand over my lower abdomen, it felt good. The hot water bottle was even better, though.

"How do you know to do all of this?" I asked.

"Ghua and Byllo and Uan. Their women are nice and tell them what they need to feel better. Some of the other females won't say."

"It's nice to tell you what we want?"

"Yes."

His unblinking green gaze held mine for a long moment. And it didn't bother me. How could it? He'd gotten me chips and chocolate and pads just to make me feel better.

I lifted my hand and set it on his cheek. My pulse fluttered at the contact and at the way his pupils rapidly expanded.

"This is the nicest thing anyone has ever done for me. Thank you, Azio." I shifted my gaze to Groth, who was quietly watching us. "You too, Groth."

He flashed a small smile at me then focused on mixing.

Azio's hand covered mine, and he pressed my palm more firmly against his cheek. My stomach dipped when he closed his eyes and simply held my hand there for a moment.

"What else have they told you?" I asked softly.

CHAPTER SIXTEEN

AZIO OPENED HIS EYES AND RELUCTANTLY RELEASED MY HAND.

"Every woman's period is different. But the best thing we can do is pay attention and keep asking if there is anything we can do to help make it better."

"That's pretty good advice. But you know you don't have to cater to me, right? I'll still stay here even if you didn't do all of this stuff."

His expression grew guarded.

"I want to care for you. And maybe touch you?"

"Your hand on my stomach did feel good. It was nice and warm."

"Eden likes that too. When the cramps are the worst, she lets Ghua lick her pussy in the shower."

I could feel my face flushing.

"Eden didn't think it was a good idea at first either. But it took her pain away. She liked it so much she begged Ghua to do it twice more and rode his face like a pony." A sexy smirk briefly flitted over Azio's lips. "If you would like to ride my face to relieve your pain, I am willing."

My face felt like it was on fire.

"I'll keep that in mind, but the water bottle should do the trick for now."

He grunted.

"Angel's breasts get sore. She taught Shax how to give her a massage. It's not sex. It's comfort. No playing with nipples. Only rubbing the swollen tissue."

A boob rub that didn't lead to sex sounded kind of nice, but after the shower story, I wasn't confident his motives were purely altruistic.

"I'll let you know if I need one," I said

A smile parted his lips, giving me a wide display of wickedly pointy teeth. He quickly smothered it at my startled expression, and I immediately felt guilt.

"I'm sorry, Azio. I shouldn't have reacted like that. Not after I saw Solin's teeth. I think I just forgot because you hide them so much."

He blinked at me.

"You want me to smile more?"

His uncertainty and willingness to be anything I needed struck a chord in me. Hadn't that been what I'd done for Wayne? Gave up my hopes and dreams to make him happy and, in the end, only made myself miserable. And I would have stayed if Wayne hadn't thrown the ring at me, oblivious to how much I was giving up for him. I didn't want to put Azio in the same situation.

"I want you to be yourself around me. If you want to smile more, then do it. If you don't want to wear those undersized shirts, then don't. I don't want you to change for me. Open and honest, okay?"

He grunted, studied me for a moment, then removed his shirt.

The easy-on-the-eyes ab display distracted me nicely, and remembering his invitation, I reached out to run my hand over his arm.

"Shirtless is a good look for you," I said. "I didn't realize what I was missing out on."

He flashed another smile my way and turned to pick up a few books, giving me an amazing view of his back. And the numerous, large scars crisscrossing it. I feathered my fingers over a few, and he stilled.

"What are these from?" I asked.

"A hellhound. It was trying to get to Cassie and her baby. Molev, Bauts, and I held it back while others removed its heart."

Azio had risked his life to save a woman and her baby. Based on the scars, that had happened a while ago. How was he still single?

"Do you want to see the books I have?" he asked, not moving to dislodge my touch.

"Sure." I withdrew my hand, and he turned toward me, showing me the "man books" he'd mentioned. They weren't books for men, like I'd assumed, but books that had a man's chiseled torso clearly displayed on the cover. Romance novels. I had my period, and he'd run out to find me romance novels.

I'd died and gone to heaven. And I never wanted to leave.

"You've done so much to learn how to pamper a woman. How would a woman pamper you?" I asked, needing to pay back some of his kindness.

"Cheri sometimes lets Farco lick her pussy while she's reading. I would like that."

I barely withheld my snort.

"So you'd consider any form of sexual activity pampering?"

He looked thoughtful for a moment.

"And touching. Your fingers are so soft."

"Okay. How about you sit here then?" I patted the floor beside the couch and took one of the books he offered.

He settled in. Groth joined us and started a movie. While I read, they watched a movie, and I played with Azio's hair.

The cramps grew worse, as I knew they would, and I broke into my chips to self-soothe. Azio leaned farther back so I didn't have to reach as far when I finished my snack. Based on the way he tipped his head, he loved having me run my fingers through his hair. I wasn't sure what the grunt meant every time I accidentally brushed the tip of his ear, though.

Distracted, I set the book on my chest and ran my fingers along the top edge of the ear, following it from base to tip.

He glanced back at me, his pupils completely dilated.

"I like that," he said simply.

"Then I'll keep doing it," I said with a smile.

He faced the movie, and I picked the book up again, idly playing with his ear. The story held my attention till the end of the movie when Azio abruptly stood.

"Is there anything I can get you?" he asked.

"No. Thank you, though," I said, finishing the page.

When I looked up, Azio was already gone, and Groth was watching me closely.

"I promise I'm okay."

"Would you like to watch another movie?"

"Please. I need to use the bathroom first, though."

He grunted and stood. Reluctantly, I did the same. Cramps tugged at my middle with increasing strength, and I made my way up the stairs, already thinking that I should bring some pads downstairs with me so I could use the guest bathroom.

I was almost to the open bathroom door when I heard an odd, wet sound coming from within. I didn't stop to consider Azio might be doing something in the bathroom with the door opened. But I should have. Oh, Lord, I should have.

He stood in front of the toilet, his pants riding low on his hips, as he watched his hand furiously stroke his massive length. The bottle of conditioner on the counter beside him explained what I was hearing.

With a hiss, he thrust into his palm a final time, covering the head of his shaft with his other hand. Ropes of white dripped into the toilet as he jerked and twitched for what seemed like an eternity.

Breathing hard, he looked up, and our gazes locked.

"Thank you for touching me. Can you turn on the water?"

I blinked at him for a moment, my gaze flicking to his cum-and-conditioner coated hands before I hurried to help. He washed his hands, dried them, and tucked his still hard length back into his pants. All the while, I stood there like the shellshocked woman I was.

When he finished, I watched him take a pad out of the box and set it next to the toilet. Then, he stalked toward me.

Impossible not to do since I was still standing between him and the doorway.

"Will you play with my ears again when you're done?" he asked.

Holy shit. I'd caused this? My heart was still racing from what I'd witnessed. The sight of him, head bent as he masturbated, muscles rippling with each forceful stroke, would forever be burned into my brain. And I was... thankful for that.

He watched me, his expression hopeful, and I managed a nod.

"I can hear your heart racing."

His big hand cupped the back of my head, and he slowly leaned in to press his forehead against mine.

"Tell me you are not agreeing out of fear. I want your touch very much, but only whatever you're willing to give."

"Okay." The word came out breathy.

He pulled back enough to brush my forehead with a kiss and went back for the conditioner. Instead of returning the conditioner to the shower, where it had been this morning, he set it on the back of the tank.

"Call out if you need anything. I will hear you."

As soon as the door closed, I turned to grip the counter and stared at my red face. He'd come up here to masturbate because of a simple touch. He hadn't wheedled or guilted me into anything. He'd simply gotten up to take care of things himself.

I glanced at where he'd placed the conditioner.

And he planned to do it again.

A slow grin chased away the shock and my insides

fluttered with anticipation—a feeling I hadn't experienced in years.

Impatient to tease Azio's ear, I hurriedly took care of myself and jogged back downstairs. Well, it started out as a walk but turned in a jog on the last three steps when I saw he was watching for me. His gaze went right to my breasts, and I didn't regret the ache the extra jostling had created.

"Ready for another movie?" Groth asked, also watching.

"Yes, please."

"Are you hungry?" Azio asked. "Do you want your cookie dough?"

"Not yet."

I was looking forward to something else. The hot water bottle was warmed again, and my nest of blankets ready for me to slide in. As soon as I was in position, Azio resumed his seat.

The room grew warmer while I played with Azio's ear and read about a billionaire dominating his assistant. My core clenched a few times at a really good part, and I wondered what Azio would do if I leaned forward to run my tongue along the sensitive edge instead of my finger.

Minutes passed. The book grew steamier. My curiosity increased. I shifted position from my back to my side, scooting a little closer. His ear was right there, and Groth's view was easily blocked by Azio's head.

I smiled slightly and leaned in.

Azio moaned and turned his head just enough to give me better access. I nibbled his earlobe and dragged the tip of my tongue to the end of his ear, then gently sucked. He was panting when I pulled back and turned his head to look at me.

The hunger I saw there robbed me of breath and some of my smug humor.

"I'm sorry," I said quickly. "I shouldn't have—"

He pressed two fingers over my mouth.

"Open and honest, Terri. It will tear my heart open if you did something you didn't like. Did you like that?"

I slowly nodded.

"Then why are you sorry?"

He removed his fingers.

"I thought you were angry that I'd teased you."

"Never. I would do anything for more of your teasing."

"Even if it doesn't lead to sex?"

"Yes. I like all of your touches."

"Okay."

He grunted and stood. It was only then that I realized Groth had paused the movie and was watching me like the real-life drama machine I seemed to be today.

"I will be right back," Azio said, moving for the stairs.

My gaze bounced between Groth and Azio. Groth made a noise that sounded suspiciously like a laugh.

"He hopes you will watch again," he said.

I flushed scarlet, but rather than hide in my blanket nest, I pushed back the covers and hurried up the stairs. Azio's pants were already sagging on his hips when I joined him. This time, his moves weren't frenzied. His tight grip slid down to the base then returned to the head in a slow stroke.

Stepping closer, I took in his size. Long and thick—thicker than anything I'd ever seen—it still seemed profane to me. But my core clenched as I watched his big hands barely close around his shaft. What was it going to feel like to have that inside of me?

He turned his head toward me. I glanced up, briefly meeting his gaze before I refocused on his hands. He picked up the tempo, stroking faster and faster until he was thrusting into his palm.

My breathing was just as rapid as Azio's when he covered himself with his other hand and came in a torrent.

CHAPTER SEVENTEEN

ONCE THE DRIPPING AND TWITCHING STOPPED, I TURNED ON the water without him asking. He washed, straightened his pants, and set out another pad for me.

"I don't need that yet," I said so he would understand my only reason for coming up here had been him.

He stalked toward me again, cupped the back of my head, and pressed his forehead to mine.

"Thank you for not fearing me."

"Thank you for letting me watch."

He flashed a grin at me, brushed his lips against my forehead, and told me to come down when I was ready.

Like last time, I took a moment to cool off. However, before I went downstairs, I detoured to change shirts.

Azio groaned when he saw me come down with one of the "soft" t-shirts he'd picked out. My gaze shifted to Groth, though, who was watching just as intently.

I reminded myself that they said nudity was no big deal as I resumed my place on the couch.

"I think I might be ready for some cookie dough," I said nervously.

Groth immediately got up and scooped some into a bowl for me like it was ice cream. When he handed it to me, his gaze swept over my flushed face.

"Thank you, Terri. You are kind to be nice to me."

I snorted. "You're the one who made me the cookie dough. Thank you."

He grunted, glanced at my chest, and took his seat. Azio sat even closer to my head, almost blocking my view of the movie. I didn't mind. However, rather than teasing his ear some more, I nibbled on the dough and read my book.

True to his word, he didn't get upset or subtly try to pester me into touching him.

However, by lunch, my period was in full swing with the cramping. Probably because the dumb book kept making me wish I had someone dominating me—not really, but I couldn't stop thinking of Azio's offer. Oh, there was no way I was going to take him up on it. It was too gross. Embarrassing.

My libido disagreed.

I ignored it.

By the time the lights came on outside, I had a slight headache and just wanted to go to bed. Azio snuggled up behind me again and then did the most magical thing ever. He started rubbing my lower back. His thumbs seemed to know just where to go and how much pressure to use.

"Oh, that feels so good. I didn't even know it hurt until you started rubbing."

"I don't like seeing you in pain."

"Yeah, I don't like being in pain either."

He nuzzled the back of my neck.

"Will you let me help you?"

"You already are."

"Shower with me. It will help."

My core clenched even as I shook my head.

"No. This is good. You don't have to do the shower thing."

He chuckled low.

"You played with my ear and watched me coat my hand with my need to taste you. I want you in the shower rubbing your sweet pussy against my face."

I had to fan myself again for a moment.

"I'm struggling," I admitted. "A part of me wants to say yes—the part that was reading a romance novel all day. The other part of me knows it'll be gross for you, though. I want to stay here, in this house, with you. I want you to keep pampering me. I don't want to do something that's going to have you looking at me differently or worse, turning away in disgust."

I'd barely gotten the last word out before I found myself in his arms as he strode to the bathroom.

"Thank you for being open and honest," he said, setting me on my feet on the tile.

My shirt disappeared over my head, leaving me actually naked on top. My hands were moving to cover the top when he whisked the bottoms down to my ankles.

"Step," he said firmly, tugging on them.

"Azio, I'm not sure this is a good idea," I said even as I obediently lifted a foot and set my hands on his bare shoulders. He hadn't put a shirt back on since I'd told him to be himself.

"We both want to do this," he said, setting aside my sweat pants. "You're afraid I won't like it. I know I will. You said you needed to face your fears. Face this."

He stood and removed his pants, his erection standing tall and darker against his skin. My gaze lingered on it for a moment before I looked into his vivid green eyes.

"And if you're wrong and hate it?" I asked.

"I won't."

He turned his back on me and leaned into the shower to turn on the water. I eyed his sculpted ass and wondered what in the hell I'd gotten myself into.

"Join me when you're ready," he said, stepping into the shower and pulling the curtain closed.

My gaze darted to the door, and I seriously debated making a run for it. Then, I sighed and used the toilet before slipping into the shower with him.

"I need to wash first," I said.

My flush deepened as he watched me. When I turned my back to him to rinse, his hands settled on my shoulders.

"I can hear your heart racing, Terri. What do you fear?"

"I already told you. You're not going to like this. It's messy."

"That's why we're in the shower," he said, turning me. "The water will keep you clean to your liking."

"What about to your liking?"

He grinned at me, showing all his pointy teeth.

"Everything is to my liking."

Before I could respond, he dropped to his knees, parted my labia with his thumbs, and stroked the flat of his tongue over my clit. A rumbling growl echoed in the space. I yipped and clutched his shoulder for balance.

"Widen your stance. I need to taste more."

I didn't even think. I spread my legs the width of the tub and lost myself in the sensation of his tongue exploring my folds. He never dipped low enough to make me self-conscious, his focus, instead, holding to how I responded to his different tongue techniques. And oh, did he have technique. I was panting and mewling within minutes.

His right hand drifted over my hip to grab my ass. He kneaded there for a moment before dipping his finger into my channel from behind.

I groaned and bucked my hips into his face.

An apology rose to my lips, but he ripped it away by thrusting his finger deeper. I bucked again, and he growled. His tongue was relentless, circling my clit and making me ache for more.

"Please," I rasped. The flat of his tongue pressed firmly against the little nub while his finger curled inside me.

My mouth opened in a silent gasp, and I topped headlong into a slow, drawn-out, channel-clenching orgasm. His finger stilled, causing one last involuntary clench. He kissed the inside of my thigh and slowly withdrew.

"You were perfect, my Terri," he said, standing to hold me to his chest. "You did so well facing your fears. Allowing your pussy to clench around my finger will help. You will see. Let me wash you. Then you can sleep."

He made it sound like I'd been the one doing all the work when I hadn't needed to do more than stand there and writhe in his secure hold. And now he wanted to wash me? The man was perfect.

He continued to praise me during his gentle washing then left me alone to dry and re-dress. I appreciated the privacy and took a moment to regroup. My legs felt boneless and barely able to support my weight, and I couldn't ever remember having such a relaxing orgasm. Ever. All I wanted to do was crawl into bed and sleep.

But I doubted that would happen. I'd seen his rock-hard length when he'd walked out. More than likely, he'd be waiting on the bed, spread out like a starfish. And I wasn't bitter about the idea of him wanting some reciprocation.

After what he'd just done, he deserved it. My cramping was an echo of what it had been.

Embracing the idea of giving a little payback, I left the shirt and pants on the bathroom floor and walked out in my underwear.

Azio's hungry gaze tracked me all the way to the bed, where he stood waiting. Rather than grabbing for me, he pulled back the covers.

"Sleep, my Terri. If you have pain, wake me, and we'll shower again."

Ignoring the seductive call of sleep, I closed my hand around his cock. Or tried too. He was too thick for that.

He grunted and made another strangled noise when I gave him a teasing stroke.

"What if I'm not tired?" I asked.

He released the blanket and gently removed my hand from his hard length. Before I could feel any sting of rejection, he kissed my palm.

"I see your weariness. Sleep. You can touch me again when you wake."

This time I let him help me under the covers and snuggled back into his chest when he climbed in behind me.

The heat of the hand he set over my lower abdomen finished the job, and I slept like a baby until sunrise.

His hand soothed over the cramping pain that woke me.

"Do you want to shower again?" he asked when I winced.

I flushed and nodded.

He made a soft growling sound and carried me to the bathroom. We repeated last night's experience, and he did his best to wring every last clench from me. Panting and weak, I almost collapsed on him. He took the opportunity to gently massage my breasts, which made me moan in appreciation. Each brush of his thumb over my nipple sent an aftershock to my core.

After that, he washed me gently and was going to leave me to finish when I stopped him with a hand on his very hard length. He removed my hand and kissed my palm.

"This isn't about sex, Terri. This is about making you feel better. You can touch me when you're ready."

In awe and slightly relieved, I watched him leave. While I'd been willing to help him, it wouldn't have been on the top of my list of things to do. Eating would be. Then maybe paying him back.

Feeling a little guilty, I finished showering and got dressed. I kept the sweats from yesterday and chose another see-through shirt. Tugging it into place, I winced a little at the ache in my boobs. All par for the course as far as period progression went for me.

I made my way downstairs and smiled at Groth.

His gaze flicked to my chest then my face.

"Would you like pancakes?" he asked. Based on the fragrant scent in the air, he was already making them.

"I would love pancakes. Do you want help?"

I moved toward the island, but he waved me to the couch.

"Go relax. The hot water bottle is ready. I will bring you your food."

"Thanks, Groth."

Settling in for another day of being pampered, I watched Groth move around the kitchen before frowning and looking around.

"Where's Azio?"

"He went to retrieve the things you gathered."

I jolted upright.

"He what?"

Groth blinked at me as I scrambled off the couch and rushed toward him.

"Why would Azio do that? He knows it's not safe."

"He will be fine. He took many brothers with him to clear out the infected. They are too close to Tenacity for safety."

My brain glitched. They were going back to the same spot on purpose, knowing the infected would be waiting.

"I think I'm going to be sick," I said softly.

Groth picked me up without warning and carried me back to the couch. Then he pulled a Mom move by setting his palm against my forehead.

"You are not warm. I'll send for Cassie."

I grabbed his hand when he started to stand.

"I'm not sick-sick. I'm sick with worry. I don't want Azio to die, Groth. I...really like him."

The worry melted away from Groth's expression, and he grinned at me.

"Azio really likes you, too. He will return. He knows you need him." He patted my shoulder and stood. "I have chocolate syrup for your pancakes. That will help you feel better."

The caring giant spent the rest of the morning doing his best to distract me with chick flicks and questions about why women did some of the things they did in the movies.

As the hours passed, though, he noticed my growing worry and coaxed me from the couch to help him make lunch. I did my best to ignore the returning cramps and other aches, along with the fading daylight.

I was sitting on the couch eating my fears via the last of the cookie dough when the front door opened. Swiveling in my spot, I turned to glare at Azio.

"About damn time," I yelled.

Then I threw my spoon at him and winced at the aggressive boob jiggle it caused.

"And I want my bra back!"

CHAPTER EIGHTEEN

AZIO LOOKED AT THE SPOON HE'D CAUGHT, THEN TILTED HIS head, studying me as he stalked closer.

"Are you in pain?" he asked.

"I'm in fear, Azio. Why would you go back there? Were they waiting for you? Did you get hurt again?"

A small smile tugged at his lips.

"No, my Terri. I was not hurt. We have the things you collected and much more from the surrounding homes. I didn't mean to worry you."

"Well, you did." I crossed my arms, and his gaze dipped to my transparent shirt.

"Your nipples are darker." He looked at Groth. "She's in pain. Did you offer to massage them?"

"Of course he didn't," I said quickly, jerking my gaze from my nipples, which looked exactly the same to me.

Azio turned his frown on me.

"He should have."

Confusion replaced anger. "Uh...what?"

"He should have," Azio repeated.

"I heard you. I'm just having trouble understanding what you mean. You wanted Groth to touch my boobs while you were gone?"

"If it helps ease your pain, yes."

I laughed like a thirteen-year-old boy watching porn with his friends. The guy I was interested in—who was also very interested in me—wanted another guy to feel me up just because it *helped* me.

"I'm sorry, Terri," Groth said, looking extremely upset. "I didn't notice."

My gaze bounced between the two fey's expressions, and I realized how entirely serious they were about seeing to my comfort. It deflated my annoyance and killed the slightly flippant way I'd been handling their concern.

As crazy as it sounded, after a day with Groth, I truly did feel more comfortable with him. Even in the transparent shirt. Comfortable enough that I could deal with the boob rubs they were talking about.

"You know what? It's not your fault, Groth. I could have asked. I was too shy and worried about the rules, though. I'm starting to understand now." I looked at Azio. "I know you just got home, but would you mind helping me out for a bit instead? You're right. My cramps are back, and my boobs are hurting and add the worry I felt for you all day... well, it made me really moody. I'm sorry I threw the spoon at you."

Azio gave Groth an annoyed look, like his BFF had let him down by not caring for his woman while he was gone, and knelt beside the couch. He leaned in and brushed my forehead with a kiss.

"I'm sorry I worried you," he said. "Tell me if the pressure is right."

Then he set his big, hot hands on my chest and started massaging. I hadn't realized how much my boobs had hurt until then. Azio paid more attention to me than I paid myself.

Sighing, I closed my eyes and let him ease the ache and melt away some of the tension from the day. I didn't even care that Groth was watching and probably taking mental notes.

"Is everyone okay?" I asked, not opening my eyes. "I should have asked that first."

"No one was seriously injured. There were a few bites, but we expect that when dealing with large numbers."

I made a face, and he paused.

"The rubbing is good," I said quickly. "The reminder of the danger you were in is not so good."

He chuckled and continued to rub my chest.

"When the ache is gone, you need another shower," he said.

It didn't take much convincing to tell him that my boobs were fine and head upstairs with him. And it wasn't awkward. He washed me gently first, using it as an opportunity to rub my boobs some more, then dropped to his knees.

"I was thinking about this all day," he said, placing a kiss on my thigh. "Were you?"

I gave him an are-you-kidding-me look.

"No. I was worrying about you."

He gave me a sexy, secretive grin and pressed another kiss to my skin. His hands slid around to the front, and he parted me with his thumbs. And damn if my heart didn't give a crazy beat because I knew what was coming.

The first touch of his tongue was magic. I sighed, widened my stance…and I watched. With an expression of bliss, he lapped at me.

I didn't need to understand why he liked doing this so much, only that he did. Running my hand over his wet hair, I found the ends of his ears and bucked into his mouth. His fingers gripped my hips more firmly, and he growled.

He didn't rush the process, though. He took his time, watching my cues and slowly sliding a hand around to enter me from behind. Something about that approach hit me just right. I twitched and bent my knees a little.

"Yes," he whispered. "Like that."

I gripped his shoulders and pressed down on his finger. The next thing I knew, I had one knee over his shoulder, and another finger had joined the first. The new position changed the angle, and he could thrust his fingers more fully into me. Everything was still slow and steady. Pushing me gently closer to where I needed to be even when I jerked and twitched and bore down on his fingers.

"Please," I begged, fisting my fingers in his hair.

He pressed the flat of his tongue against my clit and curled his fingers, toppling me over the edge. My mouth opened in another silent scream.

If this was my life now, I no longer hated my periods.

I LAY IN BED, listening to Azio's deep breathing and thinking. My period was almost over, and nothing had really changed.

In the three days since Azio had returned from his impromptu supply run, he'd been amazingly attentive. Massages, oral to ease cramps, back rubs…oh, and the food. He and Groth found anything and everything my cravings threw their way.

Azio wasn't the only attentive one. Groth remained just as kind and earnest about me staying here, despite sleeping in Azio's bed every night. He thanked me every morning I wore a flimsy shirt, never leered at me, and kept me supplied with cookie dough.

And I was finally understanding our dynamic.

Groth would do anything for me to ensure I was happy and stayed with Azio. He'd proven it by giving me a massage when Azio had left for chocolate. I hadn't asked. He'd paid attention and firmly asked to help me. I hadn't had the heart to say no. Plus, I'd really wanted to know how Azio would react.

Of course, he'd been completely fine with it. He'd even thanked Groth and joined in. It could have been weird, but they didn't let it feel that way. Instead, they talked about the different foods Groth could make with the chocolate Azio had found.

I'd also learned that Groth and Azio had always been close. They'd shared a house back in their caves too. Groth was seriously happy that I'd chosen Azio and couldn't wait for Azio and me to start having sex so I would get pregnant. How do I know that? He told me. Open and honest was a little brutal at times, but it truly helped me understand where I stood.

Azio loved having me play with his ears. If I used my mouth, he masturbated afterward. Every time. And it was no secret from anyone. Groth just grinned and told me to do it more. And Azio sat closer to me to make it easier.

There wasn't a jealous bone in Azio's body, which I really, really liked. I hadn't realized how weird Wayne had been until Azio showed me what a relationship without jealousy looked like. Azio didn't care if I teased him in front of Groth. He loved every moment of attention I gave him. He even admitted he loved that I was so worried I'd thrown a spoon at him.

I was comfortable living with the pair and never wanted to leave. And more importantly, I was back to not wanting to wait for a family of my own. And therein lay the problem. I was more than willing to have sex to make a baby.

But I really wanted to like having sex with Azio too. He was just so…amazing.

"You're very quiet," Azio said, his voice rough with sleep. "Are you in pain?" His hand moved over my lower abdomen where he'd kept it all night.

I rolled in his arms so I faced him. He brushed my forehead with a kiss and started rubbing my lower back.

"I'm not in pain. Remember when you said I didn't like sex because I'd only been with a human?"

"Yes."

"What if you're wrong? What if we make a baby, and I don't want to have sex with you anymore after that?"

He chuckled low.

"I will still be a lucky father and help ease your pain during your periods, and you can tease my ears with your tongue and watch me come in my hand."

I shook my head slowly, and my chest gave a squeeze.

"You are the most incredible man I ever met." Leaning in, I brushed my lips against his. He growled and dug his fingers just a little deeper into my back, making me moan in return.

I pulled back to look at him.

"I'd like to try something."

"Anything."

Grinning at his complete willingness, I reached up to toy with his ear.

"I don't hate sex. I just tend not to crave it. At all. My period is the exception. I've really liked what we've been doing and was wondering if you'd be willing to have sex now when it still feels really good to me."

He rolled us suddenly and nuzzled my neck.

"Is this a yes?" I asked.

"Yes. Tell me I can touch you."

"However you'd like," I said. "You've done a phenomenal job taking care of me so far."

He got up and scooped me off the bed.

"A shower first."

I grinned and let him take charge. He took his time removing my shirt and sweats. His fingers lingered on every bit of skin. Kneading my breasts while avoiding the tender nipples. Caressing my stomach. Nibbling on my neck. And oh boy, could he kiss. It wasn't all tongue but nips and licks. Teasing and coaxing me to chase him.

He seemed to know just the right thing to do. Like we were connected, and he could read me.

When he stepped into the shower to allow me to finish undressing, I was breathing hard and hurried to join him. He washed me between tender kisses then knelt before me.

"Sex doesn't matter," he said, holding my gaze. "Thank you for allowing me to care for you. To love you."

I touched his face and felt my heart aching with what I felt for him. It wasn't a deep unending love. Not yet. The love I held for him was softer and more fragile. But it didn't worry me. I knew it would grow into something bigger and stronger with time.

"Thank you for wanting to care for and love me."

He placed a kiss on my inner thigh, and I widened my stance, more than ready to accept what he offered. My hands slid over his hair at the first touch of his tongue. It didn't take long before I was bucking into his hold and riding his fingers.

When he pulled away, I almost whined. Instead, he stood and lifted me, wrapping my legs around his waist.

"Here or on the bed?" he asked. "We can use a towel on the bed."

"Bed," I said since the water was cooling.

He grunted and carried me from the room where a towel already waited.

I glanced at the towel and the closed door, then flushed in understanding. Ever supportive Groth was listening.

"I want to taste you some more," Azio said, lowering me to the bed.

His lips were on me before I had a chance to think. When

I was back to twitching a few seconds later, he pulled back again.

"Are you playing with me?" I asked with a frown.

He chuckled and kissed my inner thigh.

"Never. I want you to enjoy this, and you won't in this position. It will feel better if you are on your hands and knees."

I gave him a long look and slowly rolled over.

"Are you sure this is going to feel better for me and not you?"

He grabbed my hips and lifted me to my knees, apparently thinking I should be moving faster.

"This is about you, Terri."

He ran his fingers over my slit from opening to clit and back again. It felt so good when he inserted one finger and then another. The third was a bit of a stretch, but he went slow until I was pressing back into each leisurely thrust.

"We will shower after this," he said, removing his fingers and gripping my hip with one hand.

Then he ran his cock over my slit, slicking its length before aligning the bulbous head with my entrance. It felt like a fist pressing there for a moment. Then he grabbed my ass with both hands and started kneading it, pulling my cheeks apart and pushing them together, using the moves to open me and work his cock in.

I'd never felt anything like it. He was so big, stretching me and filling me with each impressive inch. He withdrew before he was fully seated and eased in again. Each time adding a little more until I felt his hips press against my ass.

"Do you wish me to stop?" he asked thickly.

"No, this feels nice."

He grunted and started a slow assault. Each withdrawal teased something inside me until I clenched around him. He groaned and released a hip to tease my folds, pressing just next to my clit with each thrust.

"Yes," I breathed. "Like that."

His methodical pace drove me to the edge, and when I tumbled over with a soft cry, he grunted, and the hot wash of his release bathed my channel a few moments later. He didn't stop thrusting, though, until he'd wrung every last wave of pleasure from me.

Then picked me up while he was still inside me and strode to the bathroom.

CHAPTER NINETEEN

GROTH HAD PANCAKES WAITING FOR US, ALONG WITH chocolate syrup and a knowing grin, when we came down for breakfast a while later. They both tried steering me toward the couch, but I shook my head.

"Guys, I'm good. I loved the pampering the first few days, but now that the cramps are gone, I'd rather not spend another day lying around."

"Not even for sex?" Groth asked, his tone conveying his stunned confusion. "I heard the happy noises you were making. Didn't you like it?"

"I liked it just fine, you meddler. Thanks for the towel, by the way."

He grunted but still looked troubled. He wasn't the only one. Azio wore a similar frown.

"It's because I said it was fine, isn't it?" I asked.

Azio nodded.

I sighed. "That was a modest answer—something I would say in polite company. I loved what we did. I've never come so hard before. Feeling every inch of you, stretching me…filling me was divine. I hope that doesn't go away when my period ends. But right now, the last thing I want to do is have sex again. You're bigger than I'm used to. By a lot. And I'm sore."

Azio gave me a sexy smirk.

"After we eat, I can lick your pussy instead, and you can play with my ears. My cock doesn't need to be in your tight, warm—"

"I get that you like that word," I said, holding my hand over his mouth, "but it's not my favorite. Let's go with fun zone, okay? And it needs a small intermission before we do anything again."

He licked my palm.

"What do you want to do until you're ready, then?" Groth asked. "I can find more movies."

"No more movies, please," I said, removing my hand from Azio's mouth. "If all goes well, I should be pregnant within a week or two. So, I thought that if we have something to trade, I'd like to go back to my old house for more of the baby clothes they have."

Both men stared at me. I frowned.

"You need to give me a hint. I'm not sure what about that has upset you."

"You will be pregnant soon?"

"Yeah…you know, a woman's fertile window is usually fourteen days before her next cycle. I'm pretty regular between twenty-eight and thirty days. So, in a few days, my fun zone will be all yours until I stop having periods."

Azio made a satisfied sound.

"Fourteen days?" Azio asked.

"Yep. Pretty much the middle of the cycle. My egg only

lives a day or less. But a man's sperm can stay alive for days inside of me. That's why there's a fertile window. We just need to make sure there are living swimmers in me when I ovulate."

"We do not need to wait for your period to end. I will wash your fun zone with my seed as many times a day as you allow," Azio said.

"Which is why I'm anticipating a pretty quick pregnancy." I smiled at both of them, overflowing with joy. "I can't wait to add a baby to this family. Brooke was right. It will be so spoiled."

Groth started putting away breakfast, and I hadn't even managed more than three bites.

"I will find more man books. You can read while Azio licks you. Cheri likes when Farco does that. It will help keep your fun zone wet and relaxed for Azio. I can bring in a cool water bottle when Azio is finished. It will help prevent pain so he can penetrate you more than once a day. How many times a day are needed for pregnancy? Will you know when the baby is made? Can I watch to see how it's done? You will have many fey wanting to listen to the baby's heart. And we will find more chocolate for you to prevent headaches and sickness." The words tumbled from him in a rush as he moved.

I quickly stood and grabbed his arms.

"Groth, breathe." He stopped and took a deep breath like I directed. "You're panicking. Don't. That's my job. You need to be cool and steady, right?"

He grunted, but I could see in his eyes that he was creating a mental list a mile long for the baby that Azio and I wanted to make. A baby he wanted us to make just as badly. As much as I loved his attention, he really needed a woman of his own. He was too attentive and sweet not to have one.

Plus, his question about watching made me nervous. Or maybe curiously excited, which I didn't want to acknowledge.

"You should come with us to Tenacity, Groth. There are other girls in the house that you might like to meet."

His pupils narrowed, and I knew I had his attention.

"I will go."

"What will your house want for trade?" Azio asked.

"Anything that will keep them warm or from starving. Blankets. Dried goods. Canned items are fine, but they don't stretch as far. Honestly, though, they won't think the baby clothes are worth much and won't expect much for them. So canned goods could work too."

"We have many blankets from Warrensburg. Mom put them in the basement of the storage shed. We can take those."

"Perfect."

Within an hour, we had blankets packed in totes, and the same fey who'd helped retrieve them from Warrensburg carried them to Tenacity with us.

Our reception wasn't entirely welcome. Those gathered near the wall where we landed glared, and one stupid man told the fey they weren't welcome there.

After spending so much time with Azio and Groth, I saw what it did to the fey. The hurt. The hopelessness.

"Come on. Let's trade and go back home." Our group drew enough attention that Matt, the leader of Tenacity, intercepted us before we reached the house.

"Morning, Azio. What brings you to Tenacity?"

"We have blankets for my old housemates," I said.

Matt's brows rose. "Old?"

My chest tightened, and I threaded my fingers through Azio's for support. I knew everything had happened quickly, and everyone would think what they would. But that didn't make this moment any more comfortable.

"I've moved to Tolerance to be with Azio."

"Well then, congratulations to both of you. And I'm glad I had a chance to hear it from you myself. There are rumors going around that you'd been taken against your will."

I snorted.

"Absolutely not. Azio offered me a place after Wayne told me we were no longer married. I didn't realize how badly I needed a fresh start." I glanced at Azio and smiled. "Or someone who knew how to treat me right."

Azio tugged me into his arms for a hug and a light kiss to my forehead. It wasn't to impress Matt or the few people unobtrusively watching us. It was for me, and I felt completely cherished at that moment.

"Well, I couldn't be happier for you," Matt said sincerely. "And if there are any leftover blankets after you visit your old house, be sure to let me know. I know a few families who could use them."

"We will," I said.

He nodded and walked off, leaving us to travel the rest of the way on our own.

Bobby answered the door when we knocked.

"Hey, Azio, it's been a while. It's good to see you, too, Terri. Come in. Wayne's not here right now."

"That's fine. I'm not here for Wayne," I said.

We followed Bobby into the kitchen, where he and Grandma were in the middle of a game of cards.

"I was hoping to make a trade. All these blankets for the baby clothes in the basement." I gestured to the totes the fey were setting down in the living room. "I figured you could keep what you want and trade up for what you need with them."

"Absolutely," Grandma said without hesitation. "Wayne's bringing less wood back. Something about having to go farther to find trees that are already dead. I think they're cutting fresh stuff to season it for next winter, too. But a fat lot of good that does us now." As she spoke, she motioned for us to follow her. "I'm guessing things are going just fine for you then?"

"More than fine. Going to Tolerance was the best decision I ever made." I reclaimed Azio's hand, and his thumb stroked over my skin.

"Good. I'm happy for you. Sad for us, though. Things just haven't been the same with you gone."

We sorted through the blankets then went to the basement to sort through the baby clothes. I took what I thought was fair then told her she'd do well to trade the rest to fey since they were very interested in having families someday.

"Is that why you want the baby clothes? Are you thinking of starting one of your own?"

I smiled, letting the joy I felt show.

"We are."

"Congratulations then." She smiled, but she looked more worried than happy.

"I left Tolerance's wall, you know. To see what it's like out there. To face my fears. It's not pretty. The infected are still there and want their due. They're smart, just like Bobby and Bram say they are. But with the fey, there's hope. We can't keep living like there's not. Every fey here kept me safe, and I know they'll keep any children I'm lucky enough to have safe too."

Her smile widened.

"That's good to know. Think any of them are into silver surfing?"

"Grandma!" Bobby yelled with a groan.

She winked at me.

"The itch never dies. It just needs to be scratched less frequently."

"I'm done." Bobby ran out of the basement, and I laughed with Grandma.

When we had three totes full of various baby clothes, we headed upstairs with our haul.

Abi, Danielle, and Greyly were just coming in. The little girl's eyes went wide at the sight of the fey, and she hid behind Abi's legs.

"Abi. Danielle. This is Groth, one of my new housemates." I glanced at Azio. "And this is Azio. My…"

I wasn't sure what to call him. A boyfriend label seemed a little weak since we were already talking about making a baby together. But "husband" seemed too fake or staged, considering I'd just left mine.

"Azio is my forever," I said.

He leaned in and brushed a kiss on my forehead. "And you are mine."

"That's really nice, Terri. I'm happy for you," Danielle

said. Her gaze shifted between me, Groth, and Azio. "I didn't realize they share houses over there too."

"Some do. Some don't. It depends on the fey, I think. I'm glad Azio and Groth live together, though. It's more fun with three of us."

The door had opened for the last part, and with an angry expression, Wayne entered the kitchen.

"You make me sick, Terri. I didn't believe what they were telling me. Fucking one isn't bad enough? You need to fuck two?"

Groth growled, and I grinned.

"No. Just the one. He's more than enough for me. The rest are here because they're genuinely nice people. Something you used to be a long time ago."

He shook his head at me. "I don't even know you anymore."

"I'm starting to wonder if you ever did. I'm happy, Wayne. I hope you can eventually find happiness, too."

I looked at Azio, who was glaring at Wayne. "His loss is your gain. Are you ready to take me home?"

Azio grunted and picked me up bride style in front of my ex.

"Are you still sore?" my handsome grey fey asked.

"Nope. I think I'm ready to practice again."

Grandma laughed, and Wayne swore under his breath as we left my old home. The fey surrounded us like we were out on a supply run again, and I snuggled close to Azio, loving the way they protected me.

"You really are the best thing that's ever happened to me."

"I love you, Terri. I will always care for you and any babies you allow me to help create."

I leaned up and pressed my lips against his neck, my libido kicking into high gear.

"I think you need to run home faster, so we can get started on the practicing. My Azio."

He growled at the sound of that, his lips curving into a smile, and jumped the wall for home.

EPILOGUE

AZIO'S TONGUE SLICKED THROUGH MY FOLDS WITH SLOW deliberation, and I clutched his hair, lifting my hips in a silent request for me. He chuckled and untangled my fingers.

"So greedy."

He flipped me onto my knees, running his hand over the slight bump in my stomach as he entered me from behind.

I groaned at the steady invasion of his thick length.

"I don't want slow," I said, pushing back on him. "I want fast."

"Greedy," he repeated. But he picked up the pace, his hand firmly on my hips, directing the smooth slide. My channel throbbed and twitched with the growing orgasm.

"Please, Azio. I need it harder."

He grunted and jolted me back just hard enough that his balls slapped my clit.

"Yes," I breathed.

He set a steady pace, hitting all the right spots again and again until I toppled over the edge with a loud moan. A moment later, his rhythm faltered, and I felt him jerk inside of me.

He grunted and continued to ring every last ounce of pleasure from me. Then he rolled us to our sides without withdrawing. While he gently stroked my folds, he slowly started thrusting again. It was the encore that I always needed these days.

At five months, I was ravenous for sex. And cuddles. And kisses. And everything that was Azio. My fears that I wouldn't enjoy sex with him were completely unfounded. He continued to prove that the partner had been the problem, and he had been the solution.

His girth glided through my folds, caressing every nerve and coaxing more pleasure from me.

The second orgasm rolled through me slowly, and he came a few minutes later. He kissed my shoulder and nibbled his way up my neck while I caught my breath.

"The sounds you make are beautiful, my Terri. You shouldn't quiet them."

I snorted.

"I'll use words to tell everyone how happy you make me. I'm sure Groth hears enough as it is."

Azio grunted and trailed his fingers over the first grey spot I'd gotten from sleeping with him. A mark of immunity, hopefully. Not that I ever planned to test it.

"Brooke and Solin will be here soon. We should dress." He didn't pull out, though, and continued to caress my cooling skin. Those nimble fingers drifted to my breasts, where he tenderly hefted their growing weight.

He loved everything about them. About me. Especially a pregnant me.

The baby gave a fluttering kick, and Azio grunted.

"Now, we know we are done," he said, lifting me and carrying me to the shower.

"For now. We might need to sneak away for another quickie before they leave."

He withdrew slowly and set me on my feet in the tub. It was really the only clean way to handle things after two rounds. While he washed me, I played with his ears and flicked my tongue over his nipple.

"Solin said that Brooke is just as hungry for sex. He will not mind if we end the night early."

I chuckled, knowing that Azio was right. I loved being pregnant at the same time as Brooke. We could share our aches and pains. Months ago, I would have never thought we would end up close friends. Definitely not close enough to share stories about our sex drives. But we did, and I was so glad for it.

Without her encouragement, I wouldn't have known how good hard and fast could be. Or be open to the possibility of letting Groth watch. The idea still made my heart race and my face flush. I was so much more comfortable around him. I just wasn't sure if I was that comfortable.

"I know we can end the night early. But the games and company are nice too. Besides, I want to show her the crib you found. It's too perfect not to show off."

From the moment we'd known I was pregnant, I started sharing all the dreams I'd had for the baby's nursery. Azio and Groth had gone above and beyond to find me what I wanted. It was perfect now with the crib, which made the wait until the baby came even harder to endure.

They kept me plenty distracted. Azio and I spent a lot of time in the bedroom, and when we weren't in there, Groth was a sweetheart, making me chocolatey treats and giving foot rubs. I'd been sad when neither Abi nor Danielle hit it off with him. He hadn't been too upset, though. He was far too invested in the baby I carried.

Azio washed my breasts, gently rolling my nipples.

"That feels so good."

He kissed me lightly.

"Have you given my idea any thought?" he asked.

My face was so hot it felt like it would melt. But I forced myself to meet his gaze.

"I know I said open and honest, but I'm not sure I'm comfortable with just having sex wherever and whenever in the house."

"Angel allows all the fey to watch her breastfeed the baby, and many were able to witness the birth. If you are reading a man chest book and want me to lick your pussy, why do we need to move to the bedroom? It would be much easier to lift your dress while you are on the couch."

"And it would be much easier for Groth to see everything we do that way."

"No fey has been able to observe sex. We could learn much with Groth watching for other ways I could please you."

"You please me just fine on your own," I said, leaning in to lick his nipple while stroking his thick length.

He groaned and thrust into the circle of my fingers.

"I only want to learn every way to bring you pleasure, so you will never doubt that it's possible. Even when you are not pregnant."

The man had plenty of stamina to keep me satisfied, but I understood why he was worried about this. We both were. I loved sex with Azio but feared my libido would wither and die after the baby was born. I'd shared that concern with him, which is why he was being insistent about his request.

He kissed me hungrily, thrusting into my hand, before bathing my stomach with another release.

"I love you," I whispered when he set his forehead to mine. "I'm not against displays of affection in our own home. I meant what I said about sharing, though. One fey is enough for me."

"I love you, Terri. And I will never share you."

"You are the sweetest man ever. Next time I'm horny, I'll try not to drag you away to the bedroom, and we'll see how things go. No promises, though, if you two make things weird."

"Never. Wash. I need to share the good news with Groth. He will help us end the night early so he can watch."

My core gave an involuntary clench at the thought.

When we finished with our shower, I slipped into a cute maternity dress Azio had found for me and went downstairs to set the table out on the patio. Outside, summer's warmth enveloped me, and I soaked it in.

A cat meowed and came sauntering up to me.

"Hello, Pretty Kitty. Does Tasha know you're out begging for food again?"

The door opened behind me.

"Terri, you are the kindest female I know. Thank you for allowing me to witness Azio sinking his—"

My hand covered his mouth, and he blinked at me. Behind him, Azio grinned at me.

"I'm fine with you both gaining knowledge. And I'm fine with you sharing that knowledge. But not all humans will appreciate what I'm about to allow as much as you do. So, perhaps, it's best not to announce it for the world to hear, or I'll need to end it before it starts. Anonymity is the key. Do you understand?"

They both nodded. I smiled and removed my hand.

"Good. Everything is set out here. As soon as our company arrives, we're going to enjoy time with our friends and not rush them."

The pair of them went back inside to check on the food, and I bent down to pet the cat.

My life before the earthquakes had been filled with hopeful dreams. Some had been crushed. Some I'd been working hard to fulfill.

All those dreams were my reality now. A family. A good home with two people who meant the world to me...in different ways. Friends that mattered. And most of all. Azio. The love of my life.

And I was living. Really living. Even at the end of the world.

I couldn't wait to see what the future had in store for us.

AUTHOR'S NOTE

After the overwhelming response to Demon Design, I sat down and started the next "audio pot" novella (more info about that below). Don't worry. I kept to my writing schedule for the main series and filled in idle time (aka when I stay up too late) with Terri and Azio's story.

This one isn't as light hearted, but I hope you enjoyed seeing some of the same characters. And for everyone who wants to punch Wayne in the balls...don't worry, you'll see him again in Demon Fall. ☺

Just like with the last novella, all the proceeds from this one will go toward the "audio pot" for the Resurrection series. As of writing this note, we are so close to the $2k goal needed to produce Demon Escape's audio. I've even polled my fans in the MJ Haag Facebook group to see who they'd like to see narrate Eden. It should be fun!

All proceeds from this book will be used to bring the next book in the Resurrection series, Demon Deception, to audio (it's a cost prohibitive endeavor). As before, this book was posted for free via weekly chapters in my fan Group.

Newsletter subscribers were also notified that they could/can download it for free via the book-extras link on my website. For those reluctant to exchange their email address for some free reading material, the book can also be purchased directly from Amazon or read via Kindle Unlimited.

Whatever method you chose, I hope you enjoyed this additional glimpse into the Resurrection world. I have a few more ideas if this one resonates well!

Be sure to subscribe for my newsletter via my website mjhaag.melissahaag.com/subscribe so you keep up on all my writing news. I only send monthly, so I won't spam your inbox.

Until next time, happy reading!

Melissa

THE
RESURRECTION
CHRONICLES

Humor, romance, and sexy dark fey!

BOOK 1: DEMON EMBER

In a world going to hell, Mya must learn to accept help from her new-found demon protector in order to find her family as a zombie-like plague spreads.

BOOK 2: DEMON FLAMES

As hellhounds continue to roam and the zombie plague spreads, Drav leads Mya to the source of her troubles—Ernisi, an underground Atlantis and Drav's home. There Mya learns that the shadowy demons, who've helped devastate her world, are not what they seem.

BOOK 3: DEMON ASH

While in Ernisi, cites were been bombed and burned in an attempt to stop the plague. Now, Marauders, hellhounds, and the infected are doing their best to destroy what's left of the world. It's up to Mya and Drav to save it.

BOOK 4: DEMON ESCAPE

While running from zombies, hellhounds, and the people who kept her prisoner, Eden encounters a new creature. He claims he only wants to protect her. Eden must decide who the real devils are between man and demon, and choosing wrong could cost her life.

BOOK 5: DEMON DECEPTION

Grieving from the loss of her husband and youngest child, Cassie lives in fear of losing her remaining daughter. To gain protection, Cassie knows she needs to sleep with one of the dark fey and give him the one thing she isn't sure she can. Her heart.

THE
RESURRECTION
CHRONICLES

The apocalyptic adventure continues!

BOOK 6: DEMON NIGHT

Angel's growing weaker by the day and needs help. In exchange for food, she agrees to give Shax advice regarding how to win over Hannah. If Angel can help make that happen, just maybe she won't be kicked out when her fellow survivors find out she's pregnant.

BOOK 7: DEMON DAWN

In a post-apocalyptic world, Benna is faced with the choice of trading her body and heart to the dark fey in order to survive the infected.

BOOK 8: DEMON DISGRACE

Hannah is drinking away her life to stanch the bleeding pain from past trauma. Merdon, a dark fey with a violent history, relentlessly sets out to show her there's something worth living for.

BOOK 9: DEMON FALL

June never planned to fall in love. She had her eyes on the prize: a career and independence. Too bad the world ended and stole those options from her. Maybe falling in love had been the better choice after all.

THE BEASTLY TALES

Beauty and the Beast with seductively dark twists!

BOOK 1: DEPRAVITY

When impoverished, beautiful Benella is locked inside the dark and magical estate of the beast, she must bargain for her freedom if she wants to see her family again.

BOOK 2: DECEIT

Safely hidden within the estate's enchanted walls, Benella no longer has time to fear her tormentors. She's too preoccupied trying to determine what makes the beast so beastly. In order to gain her freedom, she must find a way to break the curse, but first, she must help him become a better man while protecting her heart.

BOOK 3: DEVASTATION

Abused and rejected, Benella strives to regain a purpose for her life, and finds herself returning to the last place she ever wanted to see. She must learn when it is right to forgive and when it is time to move on.

TALES OF CINDER

Be careful what you wish for...

PREQUEL: DISOWNED

In a world where the measure of a person rarely goes beneath the surface, Margaret Thoning refuses to play by its rules. She walks away from everything she's ever known to risk her heart and her life for the people who matter most.

BOOK 1: DEFIANT

When the sudden death of Eloise's mother points to forbidden magic, Eloise's life quickly goes from fairy tale to nightmare. Kaven, the prince's manservant, is Eloise's prime suspect. However, when dark magic is used, nothing is as simple as it seems.

BOOK 2: DISDAIN

Cursed to silence, Eloise is locked in the tattered remains of her once charming life. The smoldering spark of her anger burns for answers and revenge. However, games of magic can have dire consequences.

BOOK 3: DAMNATION

With the reason behind her mother's death revealed, Eloise must prevent her stepsisters from marrying the prince and exact her revenge. However, a secret of the royal court strikes a blow to her plans. Betrayed, Eloise will question how far she's willing to go for revenge.

Made in the USA
Las Vegas, NV
21 December 2023